SPOOK HOLLOW

REVENGE OF THE NIGHTMARE JACK-O'-LANTERN

W. H BAILEY

Published by High Four Publishing

Paperback ISBN: 979-8-9931939-0-8

eBook ISBN: 979-8-9931939-1-5

Cover design by GetCovers

First Edition

For the wonderful students, teachers, and staff of
Montcalm Elementary School in Rock, WV.
The community that lovingly inspired
"Spook Hollow."
GO GENERALS!

CHAPTER ONE

SIXTH-GRADER NOAH JAMES LAY completely still in her bed. Eyes wide, breath quick and shallow, covers and unicorn comforter pulled over her head like a monster shield. The blankets prickled her face like a thousand tiny spider legs.

Beside Noah, her best friend Jeannie O'Brien stirred softly. She was sound asleep, clueless that something was watching them.

She didn't want to look.

She *really* didn't want to look.

But of course, she had to look.

She slid the blanket down just enough to free one eyeball and peek out.

The room was dark, except for the spooky orange light creeping in through the window. The glow pulsed, brightening and dimming in a slow, steady rhythm.

She held her breath as Jeannie tossed and turned, then flopped one leg over Noah, pinning her. She couldn't run away now if she wanted to.

The creepy jack-o'-lantern was still there.

Same crooked smile.

Same rows of teeth so sharp and pointy she imagined them chomping through the window glass.

Same dead, glaring eyes.

She'd never been afraid of jack-o'-lanterns, or pretty much anything Halloween, but this one terrified her.

It hadn't moved since she first spotted it an hour ago, but it hadn't been there at all when her mom chased her twin brother from under her bed.

Like most nights, especially when Jeannie slept over, Nate had been waiting to scare them. He should have learned better by now. One time, when he grabbed Noah from behind, she threw her head back so hard she busted his nose.

"That'll teach you," their dad had said. "Noah doesn't play around when she gets scared."

But this didn't seem like one of Nate's usual pranks. For an hour, those eyes had been there. Waiting. Watching. Staring. And despite the warm air flowing from the furnace vents, the temperature in the room felt twenty degrees cooler.

She pulled the blanket back over her head and squeezed her eyes shut.

When she opened them, she was standing in the memory garden between their house and her father's church.

The grass was slick with dew and cold against her bare feet. The air reeked of sour puddles and dead marigolds. Through the kitchen window, a warm yellow light glowed behind the curtains. As the fog closed in around the house, it seemed to drift farther and farther away, like she was seeing it through the wrong end of binoculars.

A cool breeze rattled tree-branch skeletons over her head. Crumbling flower petals skittered across the pathway like angry red spiders. The wooden bench swing creaked gently beneath the old oak tree at the center of the garden.

There it sat, the jack-o'-lantern, perfectly centered on the swing. Waiting for her.

Same dead, glaring eyes.

Same rows of pointy teeth. *What's that dripping from them?*

As her heart pounded harder, the fire inside the pumpkin grew brighter, blazing like a campfire, casting sharp-edged shadows that swayed with every slow movement of the swing.

The fog crept behind Noah, forcing her onward, closer to the pumpkin face. She tried to resist, but jagged gravel crunched beneath her feet with each involuntary step. She'd walked the path a thousand times, but something was off. The stones were too dark, too wet, like the thick, dark liquid oozing between the pumpkin's teeth.

The swing rocked violently, creaking back-and-forth. Its frantic rhythm matched the pounding in her chest.

She stopped a few feet from the swing. Just off-center from the pumpkin's dead-eyed stare.

The horrible eyes narrowed as it turned to face her. It knew she was there.

The wind died. All the normal sounds were gone. No fall bugs, no night birds, no distant traffic. Nothing but the hammering of her heart and the creak of the swing reached her ears.

The jack-o'-lantern's grin widened, stretching the carved corners of its mouth into a nightmarish smile.

The shadowy goo dripped onto the ground, swallowing the gravel beneath her feet.

Noah opened her mouth to yell for her parents, for Jeannie, even for Nate, but only a faint, croaking sound escaped.

She tried to run but felt herself sinking into the blackened ground like quicksand.

The swing lurched as the jack-o'-lantern rose from the seat, still glowing, still grinning. It hovered inches above the seat, then launched straight at her.

The fire behind the jack-o'-lantern face erupted into a lava flow of licking flames and pumpkin guts. She struggled to unroot herself as the jack-o'-lantern sprouted fiery hands. They wrapped around her throat, squeezing...

At some point, she had fallen asleep, only to wake gasping for air when Jeannie's arm guillotined her neck. It wasn't a killer jack-o'-lantern after all, just Jeannie flopping around in her sleep.

She squinted at the soft rays of sunshine angled across the ceiling. It was daylight, and there was no pumpkin in the window.

For several minutes she tried to understand what had happened. She finally convinced herself that it was all just a crazy nightmare. But what about the pumpkin? She was almost certain it had been in the window before she fell asleep. *Hadn't it?*

Noah lifted Jeannie's arm and dropped it.

She leaned close. "Jeannie, wake up."

Jeannie groaned as she yanked a pillow over her face. Muffled words grumbled beneath it. "Not yet, Mom. It's Saturday."

"Jeannie!" Noah threw off the pillow and shook her. "Wake up. Did you see it?"

"Huh? I'm awake. See what?" Jeannie rolled toward her, one eye open, the other clearly still not feeling it.

"The jack-o'-lantern in the window. It's gone now, but it was there last night."

Jeannie sat up and stared at the empty window.

She plopped back and covered her head with the covers. "It was probably just Nate being Nate."

"That's what I thought too, but now I'm not sure." Noah tossed back the covers and hopped onto the cool hardwood floor. She raised the window and pushed up the screen.

The morning air smelled like wet fall leaves and mud from yesterday's rain.

She leaned out as far as she could, searching the grass below. Her room was on the second floor with no porch roof, no ledge, and absolutely no way a jack-o'-lantern could have sat outside her window.

The ground below was soft and muddy, but there were no tracks.

"Come take a look," she said. "There's nothing out there."

"So, wait. You want me to get out of bed so I can see … nothing?" Jeannie mumbled into her blankets. "Can't we just go back to sleep?"

Noah didn't answer. She just stared at the ground beneath her window.

A breeze rustled the trees between the house and church. Still no tracks. Still no pumpkin.

"Not if we want to go to the corn maze. We'd better get ready."

Almost on cue, Noah's mother, Katheryn, knocked at the door.

"Girls, breakfast in ten. I'm making pancakes."

"Coming, Mom," Noah called back.

She turned from the window and stared at Jeannie, who was still a wild tangle of arms, legs, and covers. "Get up. You're the one who talked Mom and Dad into doing the corn maze."

"Yeah, but you didn't say anything about haunted pumpkins."

Downstairs, the kitchen was thick with the scent of syrup and sizzling pancakes. Nate was already at the table, scrolling on his phone.

"Took you long enough, Nozie. It's after ten."

"Shut up, Natezie." She gave him a slow, disgusted head shake as she walked past.

Nozie had been her nickname practically since birth. She hated it, but Nate didn't seem to mind his.

He grinned and pushed out the chair beside him. "Here, Jeannie. Best seat in the house."

"Better check for thumbtacks," Noah warned.

"All right, you two. That's enough." Their mother slid a stack of pancakes onto the table. With a laugh, she shouted down the hallway, "Will? Breakfast! Come and say grace so these hangry kids can eat."

"On my way!" their dad called from the study.

Noah sat at the table, watching trees sway outside the kitchen window.

Nothing seemed out of the ordinary, yet she couldn't shake the feeling that last night wasn't over.

Chapter Two

The drive to the corn maze was a quick one, only ten minutes or so. They drove past the cemetery, crossed the old bridge, and rounded the bend where blackberries grew wild. Every summer, they raced deer, bears, and raccoons to pick them.

Noah pressed her forehead against the cool glass. She watched the fall trees thin into sloping farmland and weathered barns.

Jeannie was staring through the window, too. "How come your town has the same name as the corn maze?"

"It's not the name of the town, just the valley we live in," Noah said. "This area's been called Spook Hollow for like forever."

Jeannie raised an eyebrow. "Why?"

Noah shrugged. "Just old stories. People have seen and heard lots of weird stuff around here."

"Like ghosts, or what the heck?"

"Like lights in the woods, strange sounds at night, things going missing and then showing up in random places. That kind of weird stuff."

From the front seat, Noah's dad spoke up. "The proper name is Bluestone River Valley, but old-timers called it Spook Hollow long before my dad's time. My great-grandpa said there was a Shawnee legend about a harvest spirit that protected the valley. But after years of flooding, the land went sour, so the spirit moved on. Weird, almost demonic things have happened ever since."

He chuckled. "I always thought it was just a bunch of stories moonshiners made up to keep folks from snooping around, but who knows?"

Will continued, "My granddad had a moonshine still up on Black Oak Mountain. My dad and uncle used to help him run it when they were teenagers. One night, my uncle Buford was trying to light a fire to start a batch. Every the fire caught, a big wind blew it out."

The click-click click-click of the turn signal echoed through the car as it pulled off the pavement.

"Something in those woods didn't want him to start a fire. After several tries, it attacked him, so Uncle Buford took off running for his life. He never saw what it was, but said he felt hot, sticky breath on his neck all the way home. It smelled like rotten roadkill."

The SUV crunched along a narrow gravel road and into a clearing beside an old red barn. The scent of dry cornstalks and wood smoke drifted in through Will's open window.

A hand-painted sign with dripping red letters warned:

SPOOK HOLLOW
PUMPKIN PATCH & CORN MAZE
ENTER IF YOU DARE

"My uncle and dad went up there the next day to see what they could find. They saw Buford's tracks plain as day in the mud, but no others. So, you'd better watch out for Mothman."

Katheryn laughed. "Will, stop trying to spook the kids."

Jeannie grinned. "I love it."

"Me too." Nate let out a devilish bwahaha.

Noah didn't.

A row of jack-o'-lanterns lined the path into the corn maze. Most looked harmless in the daytime, but then she saw it. One near the end had a crooked smile, sharp, pointy teeth, and dead, soul-piercing eyes. Even in daylight, it looked exactly like the one from last night. Of course it couldn't have been. That was just too weird. Even for Spook Hollow.

Will parked beside a line of minivans and pickups. The lot was filling up with families in hoodies and Halloween shirts. Kids carried plastic pumpkins while parents pulled wagons full of real ones.

"You kids go have fun," Will said, turning to the back seat. "Text if you need anything. Stay together and don't mess with the fences. And don't sneak through the corn. That's cheating."

"We've got it, Dad," Noah said, hopping out. She raced past the creepy jack-o'-lantern. She didn't look back, but could have sworn it watched her all the way to the corn maze.

Jeannie tied her hoodie around her waist. "So what's the plan?"

"Stick together," Nate said. "And if you see Mothman, run for your life."

Noah laughed. "You can't outrun Mothman."

He sprinted ahead. "Uncle Buford did. Besides, I don't have to outrun Mothman, I just have to outrun you."

The corn maze had been harder than expected, mostly because Nate insisted on leading, then got them turned around. Twice. And of course he had to jump out from behind a corn row and scare them. By the time they made it out, long shadows stretched across the pumpkin rows

Walking past the jack-o'-lanterns again, she couldn't help herself. With all her strength, she kicked the window pumpkin's doppelganger. As her foot connected with the pumpkin face, it was hard as a rock.

She'd gladly spend her whole allowance paying for it, but instead of turning it into pumpkin mush, she barely managed to knock out a single pointy tooth. For a moment, she just stared in disbelief, then picked up the broken tooth and threw it as far as she could.

As it left her hand, a fiery jolt shot from her finger, up her arm, and straight through her body. Ow! What the...? The pad of her middle finger had a long slash from tip to joint. How in the world could she slice her finger on a chunk of pumpkin?

It needed stitches, but there was no way she was going to tell her parents how she did it. She pulled a Kleenex from her hoodie pocket, wrapped it around her finger, and shoved her hand back inside.

They found Will and Katheryn near a wagon loaded with carving kits and plastic orange buckets. They were talking to the farmer, Roger O'Neil.

He smiled. "Hi, kids."

"Hi, Mr. O'Neil." Noah reached into her pocket and pulled out a twenty-dollar bill. "I'm sorry, but I owe you for a jack-o'-lantern. I kicked one. It scared me and I freaked out."

"Noah!" Will shook his head, slapping a hand to his forehead. His face turned bright red.

"I'm sorry," she repeated.

Mr. O'Neil laughed. "Which one? I don't see any smashed pumpkins."

She pointed toward the one with the pointy-toothed, now-jagged smile. "That one."

"Hmm, I don't remember that one," he said, wrinkling his forehead. "I appreciate your honesty, so don't worry about it."

"Thank you, sir. But I feel really bad for doing it."

"Well don't. It looks fine to me." He put an arm around Noah's shoulder. "But for being so honest, you kids can pick any pumpkins you'd like."

He turned to Will and Katheryn. "You've done a great job with these young folks."

"Thanks, Roger. I agree. Most of the time." Will gave Noah a wink.

The kids darted between the rows, finding their perfect pumpkins before hurrying back to the grown-ups.

"So, what are we carving this year, kids?" Katheryn asked.

Nate hoisted his pumpkin into the back of the car. "You know what I'm carving," he said. "The world's creepiest jack-o'-lantern so I can scare Noah."

Remembering last night's pumpkin, Noah's anger exploded. "Haven't you already done that?"

Nate turned to face her. "What are you talking about?"

Her face flushed. "You know exactly what I'm talking about." She stood nose-to-nose with him, one hand in her pocket, the other clenched tight.

"Noah Jordan!" Will's voice was firm as he stepped between her and her brother. "What in the world has gotten into you today?"

"Ask Nate."

Will turned to face his son. "Nathaniel? What did you do?"

Nate shook his head, eyes wide. "Beats me. I think she's lost it."

Noah tried to pull away from her father. "Oh really? I guess I just imagined the creepy jack-o'-lantern you put in my window last night?"

"I put a creepy jack-o'-lantern in your window last night? How? Your window's like fifteen feet off the ground."

"You put it on the end of a pointy stick and propped it up there or something. Then you took it down this morning."

Nate's expression gave him away. He had no poker face, but she couldn't tell if he was busted or just filing the idea away for later.

"Noah, I swear, I didn't—"

"Like you didn't scare us in the corn maze just now? Save it, jerkface." Noah climbed into the car and didn't say another word while the others finished loading the pumpkins and carving kits.

Jeannie slid into the middle seat like a referee keeping the twins apart.

The ride home was quiet. No one brought up the argument, and no one mentioned the jack-o'-lanterns. Nate scrolled on his phone as if nothing had happened. Katheryn hummed along to the radio. The usual stuff.

Noah sat staring out the window.

Orange and gold trees blurred past as the road flickered between shadow and light. She couldn't stop thinking about how solid the pumpkin face felt when she'd kicked it. Her throbbing finger made sure of that.

She hadn't meant to get so mad. She loved her brother more than almost anyone, but he drove her crazy this time of year, always trying to scare her.

Maybe he really was telling the truth, and maybe it was just a creepy dream. But dreams didn't leave you this tired, and didn't make your heart do cartwheels in your chest.

They turned off the main road, bumped past the dead blackberry bushes and crossed the old wooden bridge. Back at home, the porch light glowed by the front door, normal and safe.

Noah followed Jeannie to the kitchen while her dad and Nate carried in the pumpkins. The smell of maple syrup still hung in the air as Noah dropped her hoodie on the countertop.

She swapped the Kleenex around her finger for a couple of Band-Aids. Her eyebrows scrunched when she saw how little blood there was. A cut that deep should have bled like crazy.

Glancing at her bandaged finger, Nate laughed and raised his hand. "High four."

"How about a high one?" Noah balled her uninjured hand into a fist.

Her mother's voice rang out. "Noah Jordan James."

"Sorry." She walked away, glaring at her brother.

After a quiet dinner, Nate disappeared upstairs before anyone else had finished eating. Noah stabbed at her dinner, hoping he hadn't sulked off because she lost it at the pumpkin patch. She was sorry for getting snappy, he just made her so darn mad.

At bedtime, Noah had a hard time falling asleep. Her finger throbbed like crazy. As she and Jeannie finally drifted off, a rustle from the other side of the room jolted them awake. In the dim glow of the night-light, the closet door slowly creaked open.

Jeannie squealed.

Noah tossed back the covers and leaped out of bed. She stomped to the closet and reached inside. A startled screech rang out. "Ow, ow, ow…"

Their parents ran into the room and flipped on the overhead light. When Will saw Noah dragging Nate out of the closet by his ear and Jeannie trembling, with only her eyes showing above the blankets, he lowered his head and sighed.

"Nathaniel Joseph James," Will growled. "How many times do I have to tell you to stop scaring the girls?"

"Ow, sorry, girls! Ow!"

Katheryn stood in the doorway, covering her mouth and trying not to laugh. After Will led Nate from the room, she came inside and turned off the light. "Love you, girls. Get some sleep."

Yeah, right. Like that was going to happen.

Chapter Three

Sunday mornings at Bluestone Valley Church smelled like coffee and fresh flowers—mums this time of year. Noah sat in the second pew with Jeannie, fighting a yawn as the congregation filed in around them.

She'd actually slept through the night despite Nate's scare and her throbbing finger. Not having creepy pumpkin nightmares helped, but for some reason, she was still exhausted.

"I enjoy going to church with your family." Jeannie leaned closer. "Mine only goes on Easter and Christmas."

"It's pretty great." Noah smiled. "Dad keeps the sermons short and tells funny stories."

Katheryn slid into the pew beside them, smoothing her dress and giving the girls a stern look that clearly said,

"No talking during service." She handed each of them a bulletin and a piece of peppermint candy.

Nate was up front, helping with the communion table. When he saw Noah, he crossed his eyes and stuck out his tongue. Despite everything that had happened yesterday at the corn maze, she had to bite her lip to keep from giggling.

Everyone stood for the opening hymn. Noah was looking forward to hearing what her father had to say. Maybe it was because she was in a better mood today, or maybe it was because the whole pumpkin thing seemed settled.

Will stepped up to the podium, looking comfortable and confident in his gray suit and burgundy tie. He smiled at the congregation. His eyes paused on his family.

"Good morning," he said, his voice carrying easily through the sanctuary. "Since we'll cut next Sunday's service short for the harvest festival, I want to acknowledge that Halloween is coming up a week from Friday. I know some of our young people are already getting excited about costumes and candy."

A few kids in the congregation stirred, but Mrs. Henderson shook her head disapprovingly from across the aisle.

"Now, I know some folks have strong feelings about Halloween." Will raised his hand to quiet any potential grumblers. "Some see it as just a fun evening for kids; others worry about its darker implications. But I want to talk about something we can all agree on: the difference between harmless fun and harmful pranks."

Noah's stomach dropped. Was he talking about her jumping Nate yesterday?

"You see, there's a big difference between dressing up in a costume and spooking your friends, and deliberately trying to frighten or hurt someone. That's just being a bully. As an old Army Ranger, we had our own way of dealing with bullies, but that's a different story for a different day. And a much different audience."

The congregation laughed.

"The Bible tells us in Ephesians to 'be kind to one another, tenderhearted, and to forgive one another, as God in Christ forgave you.' We can do that, right?"

Jeannie nudged Noah with her elbow and raised an eyebrow. Noah just stared straight ahead, cheeks burning.

"I was thinking about this because of a story my grandfather used to tell." Will leaned casually against the podium. "When he was a boy, maybe twelve or thirteen, he and his friends decided to play a Halloween prank on old Mr. Garrett, who lived alone in the hollow."

The congregation settled in for one of Pastor Will's stories. Even Mrs. Henderson perked up.

"Now, Mr. Garrett was a grumpy old guy who yelled at kids for just walking past his house and refused to give out candy on Halloween. So my grandfather and his friends thought it would be funny to carve a super scary jack-o'-lantern and put it in Mr. Garrett's bedroom window to give him a fright."

Noah's hands went cold. A jack-o'-lantern in a bedroom window. Just like Friday night.

"They spent hours carving the most terrifying face they could imagine. Pointy teeth, angry, spooky eyes, the works. That night, they snuck over to his house and propped it up outside his bedroom window with candles burning inside."

Will took a deep breath before continuing.

"They got their scare all right. Mr. Garrett woke up, saw the glowing face staring at him, and had such a fright that he fell getting out of bed and broke his hip. He spent three weeks in the hospital."

A few people gasped softly.

"My grandfather felt terrible. What started as a harmless prank had seriously injured someone. He visited Mr. Garrett every day in the hospital, bringing him books and playing checkers. And you know what he discovered? Mr.

Garrett wasn't a mean old man at all. He was just really lonely. His wife had passed years before, and he didn't have any family. He was grumpy because he was sad."

Will looked around the congregation.

"From that day forward, my papaw checked on Mr. Garrett every Saturday. The mischievous boy and the grumpy old man became good friends. But the lesson sure stayed with my granddad: what seems like harmless fun to us might be terrifying to someone else. We never know what someone might be going through."

Noah shifted uncomfortably in her seat. She thought about how scared she'd been Friday night and how real her dream had seemed. Even if it was just Nate playing a prank, it had really creeped her out.

"Now, I'm not saying Halloween is all bad," Will continued with a smile. "Personally, I say let kids be kids, especially in a place called Spook Hollow, but what I am saying is we should think about our actions. Are we spreading joy or fear? Are we building people up, or tearing them down? Or worse, are we just being bullies?"

He opened his Bible. "In Matthew, Jesus tells us to 'Do unto others as you would have them do unto you.' If you wouldn't want someone to scare you in the middle of the night, then don't do it to someone else."

Nate stared down at his hands. Had he realized his pranks had gone too far? Or was he just bored as usual?

"So this Halloween, let's remember to choose kindness over cruelty, fun over fear, and love over loneliness."

Will opened his Bible and smiled. "Turn with me to Ephesians."

After communion, the congregation filed out slowly, stopping to shake Will's hand and compliment his sermon. Several people mentioned how timely it was.

Mr. Thompson, who ran the hardware store, nodded his approval. "That was a wonderful message, Pastor. Some of these young people needed to hear that."

Noah hung back with Jeannie while her parents chatted with church members. She kept thinking about the story her father had told. She was almost positive he'd shared the Mr. Garret story with Nate at some point.

"Your dad's a really good preacher," Jeannie said. "Even when he's basically letting your brother have it in front of the whole church."

"Do you think that's what he was doing?" Noah asked.

"A Halloween prank with a scary pumpkin in someone's window? He might as well have thrown a Bible at Nate."

Noah looked around for her brother and spotted him stacking chairs in the fellowship hall. He seemed perfectly normal, joking around with the other kids and not acting guilty.

"Maybe. But it worked, right? I mean, nothing weird happened last night."

"Exactly," Jeannie said. "You confronted him yesterday, and your dad called him out in church today. Problem solved."

In the warm autumn air, they walked home together as a family. Leaves crunched under their feet, and the mountains surrounding the valley known as Spook Hollow blazed with red and gold.

Katheryn prepared Sunday dinner while the kids changed out of their church clothes. The house filled with the scent of grilled chicken, taco seasoning, and autumn air drifting through the open windows.

"Can I help with anything?" Jeannie asked from the kitchen doorway in her jeans and sweater.

"Thank you, sweetie. You can help me set the table. Noah, would you grab glasses from the cabinet?"

A relaxing Sunday dinner was a James family tradition. No phones, no TV, just conversation and good food.

"So, Noah," Will said, passing tacos, "are you feeling better today?"

Noah's cheeks grew warm. "Yeah. I think I was just tired or something."

"Sometimes our imaginations run wild when we get stressed out," her mother said gently. "It happens to all of us."

"Plus," Nate said, reaching for the sour cream, "there's no such thing as haunted vegetables, anyway."

"Pumpkins aren't vegetables," Noah protested, then stopped herself. Why was she defending something that had obviously been a prank? "Never mind. You're right."

After chicken tacos, which Jeannie officially renamed "cluckin' tacos," Nate went to his best friend's house while the girls played Nerf football. The sun dipped toward the western horizon, casting long shadows across the backyard. In the distance, they could hear the faint, playful sounds of other kids taking advantage of the warm afternoon.

Jeannie tightened her blonde ponytail before kicking the football to Noah. "It's weird here with Nate at Mattey's."

Catching the ball, Noah teased her. "Weird, huh? I think you liiike him." She laughed, drawing out each vowel sound. "You want to daaate him."

"Shut up. I do not." Jeannie pretended to gag. "I just meant it's quiet."

"Mmm hmm." Noah gave her an exaggerated wink as she threw the ball back.

Jeannie caught it, raising her hands touchdown style. "Besides, he likes that Hilary girl who just moved here from Lashmeet-Matoaka."

Noah put her hands on her hips. "How do you know?"

"He sits with her like every day at lunch."

"I think it's more like she sits with him. But he is always looking at you."

Jeannie threw the ball gently at Noah's head. "Nuh uh."

Noah caught the ball and lobbed it back. Just as Jeannie caught it, Noah tackled her. The girls fell into a pile of leaves, laughing and looking up at the blue fall sky.

Noah picked a leaf from her hair and rolled onto one elbow. "Hopefully, we don't have to worry about that haunted vegetable tonight."

"Did you just call your brother a vegetable?"

Noah swatted playfully at her. "Stop. I mean the creepy jack-o'-lantern."

When Nate returned, Katheryn served her famous apple pie. Noah and Jeannie helped with the dishes, and Nate went upstairs to finish homework. The house felt warm, safe, and ordinary.

"Jeannie." Noah turned to face her as they loaded the dishwasher. "I know you wish your parents weren't so busy with your dad's campaign, but I'm really happy you're here."

A hint of sadness passed through Jeannie's eyes. For a split second, Noah saw the longing in them. Then, as always, Jeannie covered it with a crooked smile and a quick joke. "Even with all the pumpkin drama?"

Noah laughed. "Especially with all the pumpkin drama."

Jeannie smiled. "That's what best friends are for."

That evening, as they brushed their teeth, Noah said, "I think we can officially declare the great pumpkin mystery solved."

"Yep, case closed," Jeannie agreed, spitting out toothpaste.

As they settled into bed, Noah was genuinely excited that Halloween was coming up. No more worrying about nightmare jack-o'-lanterns. Just normal fall fun with her best friend.

She fell asleep easily, without checking the window even once.

Everything was back to normal. Or so she thought.

Chapter Four

After getting dressed for school, Noah realized her finger had stopped throbbing. She peeled off the Band-Aids and froze. The gash had completely healed. There wasn't even a scar. All that remained was a thin, bright orange streak.

"No way." She held her finger up to the bathroom light, rotating it, and pressing against the healed skin. It didn't hurt. It wasn't even tender. She flexed the joint. It wasn't even sore.

Her heart was hammering. She pressed her trembling hands together and compared the fingers. The healed one looked completely normal except for that strange orange line. She rubbed at it, but it didn't smudge. What in the world?

"Jeannie, you have to see this." She looked over her shoulder, but Jeannie had already gone to the car.

Turning back to the bathroom mirror, she gasped. Her eyes blazed with the same orange light she'd seen in the jack-o'-lantern. It flickered like firelight behind her pupils. Even her hair's copper highlights seemed to take on a weird orange shine. She blinked hard. The glow in her eyes and hair didn't fade, but now she was missing a tooth—the same tooth she'd kicked out of the pumpkin. A cold shiver creeped down her spine.

She ran from the bathroom, slammed the door, and flicked her tongue across her teeth. They were all still there. Every single tooth.

She turned slowly toward the wall mirror. Every instinct screamed, "don't look," but she looked anyway. Only her normal hazel eyes stared back. No fire and no missing teeth, but she was still freaked out. She practically jumped out of her skin when her mother honked the car horn. She ran downstairs to the waiting SUV, but didn't say a word about her reflection.

At school, Noah flexed her healed finger under the desk, almost hoping it would hurt, or freeze up, or something that would prove her healing wasn't some sort of weird magic trick. The morning marched on with the usual parade of subjects: math worksheets that made her brain feel like mush, a social studies lesson about the Revolutionary War that was really kind of interesting, and diagramming sentences until her hand cramped in English class.

Throughout the day, Noah's tongue flicked across her teeth, and she looked for eye shine in every mirror or window she passed. But her hair and eyes were just as dull as ever.

By the time the lunch bell rang, she was ready for a break. She joined the cafeteria line with the rest of her classmates, sliding her tray along the metal rails as the lunch ladies served spaghetti with meat sauce, a roll, green beans, and a carton of chocolate milk.

Noah made her way to their usual table near the windows. Nate's best friend, Matthew Marshall—everyone called him Mattey—was already there. His red hair stuck out in twelve different directions despite his mom's obvious attempts to tame it. Half the spaghetti he twirled around his fork plopped back onto his plate.

"Dude, don't look now, but here comes your girlfriend," Mattey said around a mouthful of spaghetti as Nate slid onto the bench across from him.

"She's not my girlfriend," Nate objected, but Noah could already see Hilary making her way across the cafeteria with her lunch tray. Her pigtails bounced with every step. She had the determined look of a girl used to getting her way.

"She seems to think she's your girlfriend," Jeannie said, taking a seat beside Noah. There was something sharp in her voice that made Noah glance at her. Jeannie chewed her bottom lip and glared at Hilary.

Noah had seen that look before—usually when someone cut in line or the lunch ladies didn't give her a full scoop of mashed potatoes. Jeannie was definitely not happy about something.

"Hi, Nate!" Hilary chirped, setting her tray down at the end of their table without waiting for an invitation. "Can I sit here? The other tables are full."

Mattey snorted. "Oh yeah. Way too full." He gestured toward the half-empty table directly behind them.

Nate kicked him under the table. "Sure, Hilary."

Hilary beamed and squeezed herself onto the bench next to him, even though there was plenty of space on the other side. Her shoulder pressed against his. Noah watched Nate try not to look as uncomfortable as he clearly felt.

"So," Hilary said, opening her chocolate milk with exaggerated care, "my birthday is next month, and mom said I could have a party. Do y'all want to come?"

Before Nate could reply, Mattey leaned in. "Will there be music? Can Nate be your dance partner?"

"Matthew!" Hilary's cheeks turned pink, but she was smiling. "If he wants to."

Nate's face turned three shades of red. "I... uh..."

Mattey grinned. "He would love to dance with you."

"Shut up, Mattey!" Nate tossed a piece of roll at him.

Noah had been watching this exchange with growing amusement, but when she looked at Jeannie, her smile faded. Jeannie was repeatedly stabbing her green beans with her fork.

Jeannie's voice was carefully neutral. "When is it, Hilary?"

"November twenty-second," Hilary said. "It's a Saturday. My mom said we can have pizza and play games and watch movies."

"Sounds like fun." Jeannie's tone made it sound about as much fun as getting braces.

"It will be." Hilary smiled at Nate. "You could be my date to the party."

Mattey, oblivious to the tension, was still enjoying himself. "He'd love to be your date."

Nate stumbled over his words. "Uh, maybe. We'll see."

Jeannie stood up abruptly. She'd barely touched her spaghetti. The grip on her tray made it obvious she was upset. "I need to go to the library," she announced.

"But lunch isn't over for ten more minutes," Nate said, looking up at her with confusion.

"I want to check out a book." She was already gathering her things. "See you in class."

Noah frowned as she walked away. To Jeannie, lunch was always the best part of the school day. She could talk without getting in trouble.

Even though Jeannie lived in Bluefield, she had convinced her parents to let her go to Montcalm with Noah. They'd been best friends since the first day of church preschool, so it only made sense to pester them about it. They'd agreed, but only if they didn't have to drive her, so whenever Jeannie wasn't sleeping over, Noah's mom happily made the round trip.

Hearing exaggerated kissing noises and Mattey's teasing, Noah turned back to the table as he broke into song. "Nate and Hilary, sittin' in a tree. K I S—"

"Knock it off," Nate said, watching Jeannie walk away. He looked lost in thought. Noah suspected he wasn't thinking about Hilary's party.

The remaining lunchtime was a blur of Mattey's nonstop goofing around and Hilary obviously trying to get

Nate's attention. Before the bell rang, she had worked the fall formal dance into the conversation more than once.

When lunch was over, Noah followed the crowd to return it her lunch tray.

By the last bell, Jeannie was mostly smiling again, unless someone mentioned Hilary. But Noah couldn't get her mind off the orange streak on her finger and the jack-o'-lantern tooth that caused it.

Chapter Five

Tuesday mornings at Montcalm Elementary were always the same: sleepy faces, the smell of pencil shavings, and kids groaning that the week had barely started. Noah yawned as she slid into her seat, dropping her backpack with a thud. Jeannie plopped in beside her, digging out a notebook covered in doodles and half-drawn bubble letters.

"Do you think Hilary will be back at our lunch table today?" Jeannie asked, not looking up from her doodling.

"Probably," Noah said, flipping open her math book. "She doesn't seem like the type to give up."

Jeannie's pencil scratched across the page a little harder than necessary.

Before Noah could ask what was wrong, the teacher blew into the room like a hand-sanitizer scented whirlwind. "Books away, pencils out. Let's get started with our warm-up problems."

The morning dragged by: math, reading comprehension, and a science video on volcanoes. Nate and Mattey exchanged dumb notes two rows over, earning a warning. Jeannie kept glancing at the clock.

By the time the lunch bell rang, Jeannie's restless expression had turned into determination. Noah followed her into the cafeteria, where the day's menu was barbecue sandwiches, fries, and a surprisingly good apple crisp.

They slid into their usual window seats. Mattey was mid-story about Nate gluing his math homework to the kitchen counter. Nate denied everything, which just made Mattey's story more believable.

When Hilary walked in, Jeannie stiffened like a cat spotting a stray in its territory. But instead of making a beeline for Nate, Hilary veered toward another table and plopped down with a group of fifth-grade girls.

Jeannie blinked. "Well, okay then."

"Disappointed?" Noah teased.

Jeannie's mouth flew open wide. "No. Why would I be?"

The rest of lunch was uneventful. By the time it was over, Jeannie was laughing again.

After school, Noah and Jeannie pedaled their bikes along the narrow road through Spook Hollow. They rode past familiar houses, leaning fence posts, and patches of orange and gold leaves. Nate trailed behind them with a backpack full of outdoor gear. He had a scouting campout coming up and needed to "train" for it by riding with extra weight.

"You know we're just doing a loop around the hollow, right?" Jeannie called over her shoulder. "Not the Tour de freakin' France?"

"Training is training," Nate puffed. When they reached the gravel turnoff toward Mattey's place, he waved and headed that way instead. "See you at dinner!"

Where the road narrowed, tree branches met overhead like the roof of a tunnel. Noah imagined they were riding into their very own secret hideout. As they pedaled along, a cool breeze carried the scent of wood smoke from somewhere in the hollow. Pastures stretched out like a green-and-brown checkerboard, dotted with cows that barely glanced up from their grazing.

Halfway to the old bridge over the Bluestone River, they passed Mr. Basham's place. His front porch was like a hardware store of rakes, shovels, garden tools, and the half-finished scarecrow he put up every fall. Today, the flannel shirt and overalls stuffed with straw, slumped in a chair as if it were taking a break. A round, uncarved pumpkin sat at the scarecrow's feet.

"Bet that's where Nate got his pumpkin," Jeannie said, nodding toward it.

A curtain in the front window jiggled as they rode past. Noah thought she saw a face behind it, but when she glanced back, it was gone. Probably just Mr. Basham or one of his grandkids checking to see who was on the road. Still, she pedaled a little faster until the house was safely behind them.

They stopped at the edge of a hayfield. The grass sagged in gray-brown clumps, waiting to spring back to life after winter. From here, they could see the ridge on the far side of the valley. The treeline had already shed most of its Froot Loopy colors.

A few crows marched along the top fence rail, cawing angrily like they were yelling, "You rotten kids stay off our grass."

"Race you to the bridge," Jeannie said suddenly, pushing off before Noah was ready.

"Not fair!" Noah scrambled to get her feet on the pedals. She caught up halfway down the hill. Both girls laughed as their tires whirred over the cracked pavement.

They braked at the bridge. Wooden planks rattled as they walked their bikes across. They paused in the middle to look at the river below. It rushed by in dark, muddy swirls, carrying rafts of fallen leaves downstream.

"It's kind of peaceful out here," Jeannie said.

"Yeah." Noah rested her chin on her handlebars. "I guess I forgot how nice it is here when nothing weird is going on."

Jeannie shot her a look. "Don't jinx it."

As the sun dipped behind the ridgeline, they turned their bikes toward home. The air cooled fast. Noah wished she'd worn a heavier hoodie. By the time they rolled back up the driveway, lights were already glowing in the windows.

Walking into the warm house after their cool ride, the girls caught the scent of dinner right away. Katheryn was stirring a pot of chili while cornbread baked in the oven. The smell reminded Noah of Mawmaw's house.

"Wash up, girls," she said without looking up from the pot. "Dinner in ten."

Nate stumbled in behind them, exhausted but smug about how many miles he'd "trained" with his backpack. Over bowls of chili and warm cornbread, the conversation bounced from Halloween costumes to Nate and Mattey's camping trip to whether or not Mattey's uncle really had a rabid raccoon for a guard dog.

"How can it be a guard dog? It's not even a dog," Nate reasoned.

After dinner, Noah and Jeannie sprawled on the living room floor with their homework, but mostly just talked. Nate sat at the table folding a paper airplane. Will came in from the study, holding a mug of coffee and shaking his head at the scene.

"You know, for a house full of smart kids, there doesn't seem to be much studying going on."

"We're thinking about studying," Noah said. "That's the first step."

Will chuckled. "How about you think your way to finishing before bedtime?"

By the time homework was done and showers taken, the house had grown quiet. Noah switched off the light and crawled into bed, pleasantly tired from the fresh air, pedaling uphill, and eating too much chili and cornbread. Jeannie was already half-asleep. Her hair draped over her face like a blonde Cousin Itt from The Addams Family reruns Noah's parents watched.

"It's wholesome, family entertainment," Noah's dad always said. "Not much of that on TV nowadays."

Suddenly, headlights flashed across the bedroom window. Noah's finger throbbed madly as she saw it—a jack-o'-lantern-shaped smear on the glass. She pulled the blanket over her face and squeezed her eyes closed. *Not tonight. Please?*

Chapter Six

Wednesday night brought an autumn chill that made the girls dig out their flannel pajamas.

Noah lay in bed, listening to the house settle in for the night: creaking floorboards, the hum of the furnace, and the soft whisper of wind through the oak trees outside.

Beside her, Jeannie shifted and mumbled in her sleep about math homework. It had been another long school day, ending with helping Noah's mom organize donations for the church's harvest festival. Busy, wonderfully ordinary stuff.

The past few days, things were nice and quiet on the creepy front. No glowing pumpkin eyes. No night terrors that left her heart pounding and her sheets damp with sweat. Noah tried hard to convince herself the whole jack-o'-lantern incident had been some weird combination of pre-Halloween nerves and imagination.

The clock on her nightstand glowed a soft green: 11:47 PM. In thirteen minutes, it would be Thursday. Eight more days until Halloween. Since Nate would be leaving for camp in a week, only seven more nights for him to scare her. So far, he had been surprisingly well-behaved. Maybe their dad's sermon about harmless pranks versus harmful ones had actually sunk in. Then again, maybe it was just the calm before Hurricane Nate struck.

Noah pulled her comforter up to her chin and closed her eyes, ready for sleep. Tomorrow was Thursday—pizza day in the cafeteria and art class in the afternoon. Maybe she'd finally finish the ceramic bowl she'd worked on for three weeks.

She was just dozing off when a sharp pain pulsed through her finger. At almost the same instant, Jeannie drew in a sharp breath.

"Noah," she whispered urgently. Her voice was shaky and tight. "Noah, wake up."

"I'm awake…" Noah mumbled. "What's wrong?"

"There's something in the window."

The words hit Noah like ice water. Her eyes snapped open. She found Jeannie sitting bolt upright in bed, staring wide-eyed toward the window.

"What kind of something?" Even as the words left her mouth, she knew.

"Just look," Jeannie whispered, pointing with a shaking finger.

Noah turned toward the window, and her heart sank.

The jack-o'-lantern was back.

Same creepy, dead eyes. Same sharp, pointy teeth. And the same orange glow behind its carved face, flickering like a candle in a breeze. But there was something different about this one. It was missing a tooth. Of course, Nate would somehow get the same pumpkin she had kicked at the corn maze. He'd probably been planning his revenge all week.

"Oh, seriously?" Noah groaned, flopping back onto her pillow and rolling away from the window. "Give me a break, Nate."

"What are you doing?" Jeannie whispered, still staring at the glowing face in the window. "Aren't you scared?"

"Scared of what? My annoying brother's stupid tricks?" Noah pulled her blanket over her head. "He does this stuff every year. It's just the latest drizzle from his little brainstorms."

Jeannie grabbed the edge of Noah's blanket and pulled it down. "But we're on the second floor. How could he even get it up there?"

"Same way as before." Noah yanked the blanket over her face. "He stuck it on the end of a pointy stick, and probably propped it up from the ground or wedged it somehow. You know how creative he gets with his antics."

"It's glowing," Jeannie said, her voice barely above a whisper. "The eyes are like ... pulsing."

"LEDs. Or one of those fake flame things from the craft store." The blanket muffled Noah's voice. "Trust me, there's a logical explanation for whatever he's doing out there." But as she said it, she opened her eyes. The pulsing glow lit the room, perfectly timed to the throbbing in her finger. She squeezed her eyes shut, blocking out the light. *It's just Nate being a pain.*

"How can you be so calm about this?"

Deep down, she was anything but calm. "Because I learned my lesson last time," Noah said. "He wants me to freak out and run to Mom and Dad screaming about haunted pumpkins. Then tomorrow at breakfast, he'll act all innocent and pretend he has no idea what I'm talking about. Well, not this time. This time, I'm not playing his stupid game."

Jeannie was quiet for a moment. "What if it's not Nate?"

"It has to be Nate," Noah said firmly. "Who else would it be? The pumpkin fairy?"

"I don't know, but..."

Noah's voice was patient but tired. "Remember the last time I saw a jack-o'-lantern in the window? After me and Dad called him out, it stopped. He's just had time to get his nerve up again."

Noah raised her head to look up at Jeannie. "If you're scared, you can sleep on this side of the bed. But I'm not letting Nate ruin another night's sleep with his little tricks."

"I can't believe you're just going to ignore it."

"Watch me."

Minutes passed. Jeannie shifted in the bed, occasionally whispering things like, "It's still there," and, "I think it moved." Noah refused to give Nate the satisfaction of looking.

Every part of her wanted to peek, to see what Nate had come up with this time, but she knew that's exactly what he wanted.

"You know what the worst part is?" Noah said under her breath. "He's probably out there right now, hiding in the woods, waiting to see if we'll freak out. It's worth it to him to get in trouble, so long as he scares us."

"But Noah..."

"It's just an overgrown berry with a light in its guts. The most dangerous thing about it is that we might trip over it if he leaves it on the front porch."

She still refused to look. She'd made her decision, and she was sticking to it. No more losing sleep over his goofy pranks.

"I'm going to sleep now," she announced, fluffing her pillow aggressively. "And tomorrow morning, when that stupid pumpkin is gone, we'll know for sure it was just Nate being Nate."

"What if it's still there in the morning?"

"Trust me. It won't be," Noah insisted, and mostly even believed it herself. "By sunrise, he'll clean up his mess and move on to planning his next big scheme."

Jeannie was quiet, but Noah could tell she was still awake, still staring at the window. But at least she didn't seem ready to bolt out of bed.

Noah kept her eyes closed and her back turned to the glowing orange light filling the room. She would not let Nate win.

Even when she heard soft tapping against the glass, like fingers drumming impatiently, and the light grew bright enough to see with her eyes closed, she stayed put.

And even when Jeannie whispered, "Noah, I think it's trying to get our attention," she just pulled her pillow over her head. "Nice try, but I'm not falling for it."

Eight more days until Halloween, she thought as exhaustion won out over curiosity. If this was Nate's opening move, he was going to have to step up his game because Noah James was officially over being scared of jack-o'-lanterns.

At least, that's what she told herself as she finally drifted off, ignoring the orange glow throbbing in time with her finger and heartbeat.

Chapter Seven

Morning sunlight splashed across Noah's room in a soft, golden puddle. She turned one cracked eye to the window. Nothing there but a thin smear of dew along the bottom of the glass and a faint reflection of her own messy hair.

She flexed her injured finger. No throbbing—that was good. Even in the morning light, the orange streak was still there, maybe a little larger than before.

Jeannie stretched beside her, hair sticking up like she'd wrestled a tornado in her sleep. She glanced at the window and exhaled.

"It's gone." Jeannie's reaction was a mix of confirmation and relief.

"Told you." Noah sat up. "He got bored and gave up."

Climbing out of bed, she laughed. "Nate's like the boogeyman; he loses his evil powers if you're not afraid."

Without saying a word, they came to the same conclusion. No talking about it. Not to Nate. Not to anyone. If there was no reaction, there was no fun for him.

They dressed quickly and slid down the banister to breakfast, forgetting all about Nate and the night before. The kitchen was warm and bright. Coffee gurgled in the maker, bacon sizzled on cast-iron griddle, and the toaster popped up four perfectly golden slices. Katheryn moved between the stove and the table, humming a hymn under her breath. Will unfolded the local newspaper, glasses perched on his forehead.

Nate sat at the end of the table with a jar of apple butter and a pile of toast. At first, he didn't look up. When he did, his eyebrows lifted, as if he'd been waiting for something.

"How'd you two sleep?" Will asked, still scanning the paper.

"Like a log," Noah replied, pouring a glass of orange juice. "Didn't move all night."

"Same," Jeannie added, reaching for the butter and keeping her voice light. "Best sleep since ... forever."

"Huh." Nate took a bite of toast. His expression was blank, but a suspicious wrinkle creased his brow.

Katheryn set a plate of scrambled eggs on the table. "Eat up. We're leaving early so I can stop by the post office before I drop you off."

Soon, they piled into the SUV and turned out of the driveway toward the Rock, WV post office. Frosty grass lined the roadside ditches, and leaves skittered across the pavement like little orange chipmunks.

As they drove past Mr. Basham's place, Jeannie craned her head to keep his house in view. The scarecrow had taken its usual place, in a rocking chair beside the front door. Mr. Basham had carved an oversized jack-o'-lantern face and perched it on the scarecrow's shoulders. A drawstring held an old straw hat atop the warty pumpkin head.

Jeannie's eyebrows arched. "Now that's a pumpkin."

At school, all the usual sights and sounds met them at the door. Kids chattered, doors slammed shut, and the intercom hissed as the principal started morning announcements.

"You think he'll bring it up?" Jeannie asked softly.

"Nope," Noah said. "Not if we don't. He loses interest if nobody plays along."

Between classes, Noah saw Hilary chattering away at the water fountain between two girls from another class. She gave Nate a little wave as he rushed by. He pretended not to notice, then tripped over his own two feet. Mattey laughed loud enough to earn a look from a teacher.

By lunch, the morning had taken on that ordinary school-day blur. Pizza day filled the cafeteria with the scent of pepperoni and melted cheese. Noah, Jeannie, and their friend, Winry, took up their normal seats by the windows as the rest of the tables filled up around them.

Winry sipped chocolate milk as she wrote and doodled in her notebook. She'd spent half the semester creating the world details for her epic fantasy story, The Archipelago. Noah and Jeannie flipped wide-eyed through the pages. "This is amazing. You'll be the next J. K. Rowling."

"Thanks. I sure hope so, but I'm going more for Hiromu Arakawa, since I was named after one of her characters."

Across the room, Nate and Mattey lobbed pizza crusts at the trash can. They were both pretty lousy shots. A glance from the custodian sent them scrambling to pick up their misses.

The afternoon passed like a groggy sloth. After science, the last bell rang, and students poured into the parking lot. Katheryn waved from the curb. Cardboard boxes of donated clothing and canned goods filled the back of her SUV.

"Festival prep night," Katheryn announced as they buckled in. "We'll knock out as much as we can before dinner. Your dad is stringing lights at the church."

On the drive back through the valley, they passed Mr. Basham's again. The scarecrow looked lazier in the afternoon light. Its head tipped forward as if it were napping in the sunshine.

At the church, they wasted no time getting to work. Tables unfolded with a metallic click as the fellowship hall took on a busy-bee vibe with volunteers buzzing about everywhere—sorting coats by size, folding scarves into baskets, and arranging packaged goods with their labels facing forward.

Jeannie arranged pies and breads for auction. The cinnamon and vanilla in the air made more than one belly rumble.

"Admit it," Jeannie said, rubbing her hands together. "You thought about the pumpkin at least once today."

"Only when I remembered to not think about it," Noah said.

Jeannie smiled. "You're right. It had to be Nate. No one else would bother."

"Exactly."

Back at the house, Katheryn slid a casserole into the oven. She parked the kids at the kitchen table with stacks of festival flyers and a tub of envelopes. They set up a makeshift assembly line. Noah folded flyers, Jeannie stuffed them into envelopes, Katheryn stuck on stamps, and cooked dinner. It was strangely satisfying to see all those neat little piles shrinking to nothing.

Nate wandered in with a coil of paracord and a hand-written checklist. "Have y'all seen my flashlight? The big one with the heavy batteries."

"Garage shelf," Noah answered without looking up. "Back left, next to the camping stove."

Nate gave her a look that said he was either impressed, or suspicious. "Thanks."

Jeannie looked up as she sealed an envelope. "Planning a midnight hike?"

"Outdoor skills," he said, and left it at that.

After washing dishes, the girls plopped on Noah's bed. Jeannie flipped through her phone while Noah checked her math workbook, circling two problems that made no sense. A faint bump came from the hall, the kind of sound that could be anything in an old house.

"Still nothing from Nate?" Jeannie asked, glancing toward the window.

"Nope," Noah said.

"Good," Jeannie said. "I'd like to save my heart attacks for Scarowinds."

They brushed their teeth, said goodnight to Kath-eryn and Will, and climbed into bed. The sheets were cool against Noah's legs as she looked at the window one last time. Stars dotted the night sky beyond the glass. No pumpkin. No glow. And no reason to do anything other than sleep.

She let her eyes close. Outside, something shifted in the yard. A dry hiss of cornstalks. A scuff on gravel that could have been a shoe or could have been nothing at all. If she had stayed awake, she might have noticed a dim orange streak threading through the trees, quick as a blink, then disappear back into the woods.

Chapter Eight

On Friday, the school day came and went with zero drama. That evening, after dinner and dishes, Will suggested a rematch of the last family Monopoly game. Nate claimed he only lost because "certain people" had conspired to keep him in jail.

"Certain people," Katheryn said, laying out the Chance cards, "were just following the rules. You should try it sometime."

"Which rules?" Nate asked. "Because we have at least four sets."

"Tonight it's the actual rules," Will said. "Official banker, official auction, no free parking jackpot."

Nate narrowed his eyes, already suspicious. "Can I be the banker?"

"Rock, paper, scissors," Jeannie said, grinning. "Winner gets the money box."

They threw down. Jeannie beat everyone and bowed like a queen. "Ladies and gentlemen, your trustworthy banker."

"Trustworthy banker? Isn't that, what do they call it when two words don't go together? A moron ox?"

Katheryn shook her head. "Oxymoron. Roll."

Turning to Noah, he looked stunned. "What did she call me?"

The first laps around the board were all purchases and groans. Jeannie bought both light-blue properties. She crowed about "a growing neighborhood with a strong sense of community." Noah snagged two railroads and announced she was starting a transit empire. Nate landed on Income Tax and clutched his heart like a wounded actor. He passed Go on the next turn and made a show of fanning his two hundred dollars at the rest of them.

"Humility looks good on you," Will said.

"Never heard of it," Nate replied, tossing the car two extra squares "on accident" and pretending not to notice the cocked heads and stares.

"Back two," Jeannie said, pointing. "We're keeping this honest."

Half an hour in, Katheryn drew a Chance card and had to go directly to jail. She took it with grace, rolled snake eyes for doubles, and cheered like she'd won the Super Bowl. Will bought both utilities and spent the next five minutes explaining to anyone who would listen why they were secretly the best value on the board.

"They're never the best value," Nate said.

Noah traded a Get Out of Jail Free card for Jeannie's railroad, then immediately landed on Boardwalk. She howled with laughter when it was still unowned.

"When I'm a policeman, I'll let you out of jail for free, Jeannie," Nate said, then pointed at Noah. "But not you."

The game slid toward silly. Will tipped the top hat token every time he collected rent, while Katheryn used the iron token to flatten her property deeds for luck.

As Jeannie neatly placed another row of houses, she announced the creation of a new HOA on Marvin Gardens. Nate pulled a Community Chest card that awarded him second place in a beauty contest. He stood and gave a royal wave like a pageant queen.

"Second place sounds about right. If there were two contestants," Noah said.

By the time houses started appearing on orange and red properties, everyone was punchy. Jeannie rationed out chocolate chips to players who didn't whine when they had to mortgage something. Will paid a luxury tax and accused the dog token of messing on his lawn. Katheryn yawned and checked the clock.

"Last lap," she said. "The loser clears the board."

Nate rolled a nine, sailed past Go, and landed on Noah's railroad.

"Two hundred bucks," Noah said sweetly.

"That's extortion," Nate argued.

"Not when you're trespassing."

Despite his protests, Nate finally paid up, counting out ones, fives, and tens.

Jeannie rolled a five and landed on Boardwalk. Noah paused for dramatic effect, then waved her on. "Open-house special. No rent."

Jeannie dropped her chin gallantly and brought a closed hand to her chest. In her best British-royalty accent, she said, "I shall never forget this act of mercy."

In the end, they called it a draw rather than counting everyone's assets. Katheryn set the deeds back in the box, Jeannie arranged the money with suspicious professionalism, and Nate cleared the table with a sigh that made him sound like an old man.

Everyone drifted into their evening routine. Showers hissed. Hair dryers hummed. The TV mumbled to itself before someone clicked it off. Noah and Jeannie changed into pajamas and climbed into bed, contented and tired in a way that comes from laughing too hard and arguing over rent with people you love.

Jeannie fluffed her pillow. "I've been thinking ... do you still believe it was Nate the other night?"

"Oh, yeah," Noah said. "You watch, he'll be too tired from playing Monopoly to try it again tonight."

Jeannie sounded less than convinced. "I sure hope so. Goodnight."

"Nighty night."

Noah closed her eyes, but a tiny flicker of unease tickled her spine as she drifted off to sleep. Sometime later, she awoke with a start.

Her breath was fast and shallow. The glass had been black. Now, a faint orange glow spilled in. There was no sign of the pumpkin, but its telltale light pulsed through the room. Dim-bright, dim-bright, like a heartbeat. Her finger throbbed in perfect rhythm with the pulsing.

Beside her, Jeannie's breath was slow and steady. She was sound asleep.

The light brightened, flickering across the walls and ceiling. Shadows stretched and shrank as if something outside was moving, pacing.

Goosebumps swarmed over her arms and legs. She covered her head and waited.

After what seemed like hours, she slid the blanket down to peek over it.

The pumpkin was there.

She squeezed her eyes so tight they hurt. She couldn't hear the wind or cars driving by. Only a faint, irregular creaking. She once heard you can't count in order if you're dreaming, so she counted...

One...

Two...

Three...

Four...

She couldn't remember the last number she counted, but when her eyes blinked open, she was back in the memory garden. Cold, damp grass stuck to her bare feet. The air smelled like rain-soaked graves and rotting funeral flowers. The wooden swing rocked gently as the ropes groaned with each movement.

The jack-o'-lantern sat in the center of the swing just like before. Except it wasn't really sitting. It was hovering.

Its glow cast jagged shadows over the wilted flowerbeds. The gaping, broken tooth was a sharp reminder of the day she'd lashed out. It was even scarier without it, if that was possible.

A thick, shadowy ooze drooled between the teeth and dripped from the swing, covering the ground around her feet. She tried to back away before it reached her. But the slimy goo flowed between her toes and around her feet, practically cementing her in place.

With some effort, she took a step back. The stones beneath her feet squished, wet and sickening.

A whisper curled through her head, quiet but close, like someone leaning right up to her ear. "Are you afraid?"

She barely heard her own trembling reply. "Who's there?"

The whisper came again, worming its way through her terror.

"I've been waiting for you."

As her heart pounded in her ears, the pumpkin's eyes flared.

She glanced toward the house. The kitchen light flickered on and off. The house was close enough to run to, but too far to make it in time.

The swing groaned again. Each swing was slower, but somehow longer.

Noah's chest tightened. Her finger throbbed worse than ever. "What do you want?"

The voice sounded almost amused.

"In your worst nightmares, you could never dream what I want."

The fog rolled in behind her, creeping low over the ground, forcing her through the slimy ooze toward the swing.

She tried to back away, but her foot sank into the gooey stones like Silly Putty. The air grew thicker, harder to breathe.

The jack-o'-lantern leaned forward, leaving the swing behind as it floated closer and closer. The mouth opened impossibly wide, stretching beyond the carved lines.

She heard another whisper, softer this time.

"Wake up."

She shook her head. "But, I am awake."

"Noah, wake up."

It was Jeannie's voice, but Jeannie wasn't here. She was asleep in Noah's room.

The flaming pumpkin could almost reach her now. She felt its fiery breath on her face. The stench turned her stomach. It snapped at her face, just far enough away that each disgusting chomp missed.

She tried to scream, but only single mousy whisper squeaked out.

Firelight flared in the jack-o'-lantern's mouth and eyes until the entire garden glowed orange. Two burning hands sprouted from its pumpkin shoulders. Jagged, flaming fingers reached for her. She squeezed her eyes shut, tighter than ever.

"Wake up!" The words were louder now.

Noah lurched, still unable to move, still unable to scream. The fiery pumpkin hands gripped her shoulders and shook her. Her eyes snapped open as a sharp, terrified gasp filled her lungs. Jeannie's face swam into view, hair mussed, and eyes wide.

She pried Jeannie's hands away from her shoulders. "Stop shaking me."

"Sorry. You were freaking out in your sleep," Jeannie said.

Noah sat up, heart hammering, staring at the window. No flames. No pumpkin. Only the slow sway of moonlit tree branches in the night breeze. She saw a faint, almost imperceptible orange glow winding through the trees and over the ridgeline.

CHAPTER NINE

That evening, Noah was still pretty shaken up, but determined not to let creepy nightmares control her life. Saturday nights at home were never fancy. Tonight had been leftovers, a plate of brownies that had somehow survived overnight on the counter, and a movie Jeannie picked. "It looks too silly to be scary."

The girls were sprawled across the living room rug, wrapped in blankets and laughing until Katheryn shooed them upstairs with the reminder that "ready or not, church comes early."

Nate lingered downstairs, pretending to clean up but really just fishing the last brownie from the pan. Will was working in his study. The muted clack of computer keys carried faintly down the hall. The warm, familiar smell of a laser printer working overtime hung in the air as he printed the last of tomorrow's church bulletins.

By the time the girls made it upstairs to Noah's room, the house had settled into its usual late-night rhythm. Pipes sighed in the walls, the dryer thumped once, then buzzed, and finally went silent.

"Your mom's making cinnamon rolls in the morning," Jeannie said as she brushed her teeth, toothpaste foam muffling her words.

Noah grinned around her own toothbrush. "It's a bribe so we're ready for church on time."

"Works for me," Jeannie mumbled, spitting into the sink.

They rinsed and elbowed each other for mirror space. Jeannie hummed an off-key pop song while Noah tried to braid her damp hair. In the hallway, the floorboards creaked under someone's weight, followed by the quick creak of Nate's door hinges.

Jeannie flopped backward onto the bed, stretching until her knuckles brushed the top of the headboard. Noah switched off the overhead light, leaving only the warm pool of her nightlight.

"Reading all night?" Noah asked as she laid her phone on the nightstand.

"Just one chapter." Jeannie tapped her Kindle. "Two tops."

Noah laughed. "That's what you said last time, and you ended up on chapter twelve."

"Yeah. I was hooked," Jeannie said with mock seriousness, swiping to the next page.

Noah slid under the covers, tugged the blankets under her chin, and let herself sink into the mattress. Somewhere down the road, a car whispered past. Its headlights painted silver shapes across the wall as the hum of the furnace sent a soft rush of warm air through the vents.

It was the kind of safe, ordinary night that made her want to sleep, but she couldn't stop glancing at the window.

The feeling of safety didn't last. Around midnight, she heard a thump at her window. An orange glow filled the room.

Nate's pumpkin was back; crooked grin, jagged eyes, pointy teeth, and that horrible glow from within. The light inside didn't flicker. Its flame burned constant and unwavering, as if it were staring her down. Daring her to blink.

For a long moment, she couldn't tear her eyes from the creepy, glowing grin.

Suddenly the light changed. A thin white slice cut across the glass as quick as a camera flash.

Flashlight. It had to be. Haunted jack-o'-lanterns don't need headlights.

Her stomach gave a quick jolt before her mind caught up. Now she was sure last night had just been a nightmare. A repeating, extra creepy one for sure, but still just a nightmare. Tonight, she was just as sure Nate was at it again. She pictured him crouched under her window, wearing his headlamp, holding the pumpkin on a stick, and grinning like a loon.

Nice try, Nate.

She rolled onto her back, fixing her eyes on the ceiling. The orange glow pooled over her blanket and the curve of Jeannie's sleeping face.

Beside her, Jeannie hadn't moved. Her breathing was slow, even, and deep. A loose strand of hair moved slightly with each breath.

Noah considered getting up and pulling the curtain closed. Or catching him in the act, but that would mean letting him win. He had been trying to outdo himself every Halloween since second grade, from stuffing spiders in her shoes to spider-webbing her toilet seat. She had to admit; the spider web ticked her off far less than the Saran Wrap on April Fools' Day.

Once, he'd tried to convince her the church was haunted. Mattey hid in the attic and rang the bell while the knotted rope appeared to move up and down on its own. This was just another round in the same old game.

She turned away from the window, but something drew her back. She heard a faint shhkk, like dry branches scraping against brick. Then silence. No footsteps. No muffled laugh. No whispered exchange with a co-conspirator.

Her fingers tightened around the blanket. "You're wasting your time, Nate," she mumbled into her pillow.

The glow didn't flicker. It didn't dim. It just kept burning, steady and patient. Even through her closed eyelids, she saw it.

Minutes stretched into an hour. Her mind drifted to what he'd say in the morning. How innocent he'd pretend to be. Somewhere outside, she heard a faint chuckle, then silence.

Eventually, her breathing fell into rhythm with Jeannie's, and the warmth of the bed won out over aggravation. She wrapped a pillow around her head and grumbled about putting Nate up for adoption.

In the morning, sunlight woke her from a dream about wildflowers and butterflies. The window was empty. There was only a faint smear of dew at the bottom of the glass.

She flexed her finger, half-expecting it to throb. It didn't, but the orange streak was thicker and longer than before. It had crept past the joint crease like a slow-moving stain. She stared at it, trying to remember if it had always reached that far, then shook her head. Her wild imagination was making connections that weren't really there.

She dressed for church without thinking much about it until Jeannie appeared in the doorway, hair damp from the shower.

"You slept through it," Noah said, tugging on her sweater.

"Slept through what?" Jeannie asked, pulling her brush through a stubborn knot.

"The pumpkin. Nate was at it again. I even saw a flashlight this time."

Jeannie stopped brushing for a second, eyes flicking toward the window before she went back to the knot in her hair. "You're sure it wasn't a dream? After that nightmare you had the other night..."

"I'm sure. I stayed awake for a while just waiting for him to take it down, but I fell asleep." Noah smirked.

They headed downstairs to the smell of coffee and cinnamon rolls. Nate was already at the table, drumming his fingers against his plate while Katheryn poured juice. He didn't look at Noah, and she didn't look at him.

Let him wonder, she thought, slipping into her chair. If he wanted a reaction, he'd have to work a lot harder than that.

The first crunchy frost of the season was already melting from the grass as she and Jeannie walked next door to the church. She thought she smelled burnt pumpkin and glanced back at her window, half-expecting the crooked, broken grin to be staring back at her.

Chapter Ten

Sunday breakfast was so quiet the clink of plates and glasses was louder than the conversation. Katheryn hummed along to STAR 95 FM on the radio. Will skimmed the paper, and Nate sat hunched over his plate like a caveman protecting a fresh wildebeest kill.

The first crunchy frost of the season was already melting from the grass as Noah and Jeannie walked next door to the church.

Noah thought she smelled burnt pumpkin and glanced back at her bedroom window, half-expecting the crooked, broken grin to be staring back at her.

At church, they sang hymns everyone knew by heart. Will's sermon on helping others made more than a few people glance at their kids, including Will himself. Especially when he spoke about the joys of sibling rivalry.

After the service, the Harvest Fest was a huge success. The church raised nearly three thousand dollars for charity, and as a bonus, the twins got along all day.

When they returned to the house, the smell of slow-cooker roast pulled them toward the kitchen almost before they had hung up their coats. Nate willingly said the blessing before they dug in.

Jeannie whispered, "What's up with him? It's like he's going out of his way to be nice."

Noah shrugged. "Who knows? But that's creepier than the pumpkins."

They spent the evening grazing on leftovers, flipping through phones, and doing homework. The clock ticked lazily toward bedtime. By 7:00 PM, daylight had faded to a blue-gray overcast. The roar of the fireplace and the movie playing in the background felt extra cozy as Noah and Jeannie catnapped on opposite ends of the couch. They missed most of the movie but woke up just in time for the credits.

Before bedtime, the girls were already sprawled across Noah's bed with a deck of cards between them. They played until the score sheet became more doodles than numbers, then switched off the light and let the whisper of the house lull them to sleep.

To Noah's surprise, nothing unusual happened that night. She even stayed awake until nearly midnight, just to see what sort of hijinks Nate might be up to, but surprisingly, he didn't seem to be up to any.

Until just before dawn, that is.

The first clue that something was amiss was the sound of a thump at the window. Not loud, but sharp enough to cut through the quiet and make Noah's eyes snap wide open. She held her breath, listening. A second sound followed, softer, like something brushing against glass.

"OK," she told herself. "This time, I KNOW I'm awake."

She turned her head toward the window just in time to see a faintly glowing pumpkin grinning at her in the gray, early-morning light. It swayed slightly, impaled on the end of a long stick. Its crooked mouth tilted as it bobbed left and right. She pictured Nate standing below her window, holding the stick with a goofy grin.

Her blood ran cold, then hot, as rage blazed through her body.

She was out of bed before she knew it, snatching her foam bat from the corner by the door so hard it rattled pictures on the wall.

Jeannie bolted upright, hair sticking out in every direction. "What the heck...?"

Noah was already through the door. So angry her heartbeat pounded in her ears.

"NOAH!" Jeannie shrieked, scrambling after her. "Where are you going?"

Noah stomped down the stairs barefoot, arms pumping wildly. She yanked open the front door and didn't bother to close it. Cold air bit at her legs as she sprinted across the porch and into the yard.

Nate's head jerked up as he saw her round the corner. His eyes went wide. He dropped the pumpkin stick as if it had burned him and tore off toward the backyard.

"GET BACK HERE, CHICKEN!" Noah shouted, waving the foam bat over her head like a caveman. She would never actually hit him, even with a harmless foam bat, but he didn't need to know that.

"YOU'RE CRAZY!" Nate hollered over his shoulder.

Behind her, Jeannie's voice cracked in panic. "NOAH, PUT DOWN THE BAT!"

The frosty grass crunched beneath Noah's bare toes, burning them. The chase looped around the house, past the driveway, and into the churchyard. Nate's laughter carried back to her: breathless, high-pitched, and edged with just enough fear to make her run even faster.

He tripped on the edge of the sidewalk and went down hard, palms smacking the concrete. Noah closed the gap in two strides and pointed the bat at him like she was aiming for the cheap seats. Before she decided what to do now that she'd actually caught him, her father's voice cracked through the cool morning air like a whip.

"NOAH JORDAN JAMES!"

Will sprinted across the yard in his pajamas. Katheryn was right behind him in her robe. Jeannie skidded to a stop beside them, panting.

"Have you lost your everloving mind?" Katheryn demanded, eyes flicking from Noah's bare feet to the bat.

"No! Nate lost his. He's been messing with me for days, and I'm sick and tired of it!"

Noah was so angry she could hardly breathe. "The pumpkin in the window? The flashlight? The thumping on the siding? All him!"

"Just this once!" Nate protested, scrambling backward on his elbows. "I didn't do any of that other stuff!"

Noah let out a sharp, disbelieving laugh. "Liar! I guess your pumpkin looking just like the one at Mr. O'Neil's is just a coincidence?"

"It is. Kinda!" Nate's voice cracked as he tried to get to his feet.

Will stepped between them, one hand reaching for the bat. "Enough. Both of you." He pried it from Noah's grip with a firm tug. "Nate, get inside. Noah, you too."

Nate pushed himself up, mumbling something about Noah having no sense of humor.

"Can it, Nate. You'd be grounded for life right now if we hadn't already paid for scout camp," Will said over his shoulder as he stomped back to the house.

"And Noah, so would you for trying to brain your brother."

"He doesn't have a brain." Behind her parents' backs, she kicked at Nate, but he sidestepped out of range.

Her tight jaw, pounding heart, and burning feet were a brutal reminder of just how far past her limit this whole pumpkin ordeal had pushed her. Out of the corner of her eye, she spotted the jack-o'-lantern lying in the yard where Nate had dropped it.

Even in the early-morning light, it wasn't scary at all. The carved edges were blackened inside. A faint curl of smoke drifted from its jagged grin. A faint smell reached her before she realized she'd stopped walking. It was sharper than candle wax. Charred pumpkin.

She ran to it, sprang high into the air, and stomped it with both bare feet. The brittle shell imploded with a sick, wet crunch. Bits of rind and pulp flew in every direction. A crooked eye stared up blankly from the frosty grass. That would put an end to Nate's pumpkin pranks.

She didn't say a word. She just wiped her eyes and went inside to get ready for school. The whole family knew when Noah got so angry she cried, it was best to steer clear. And today, she was crying.

Chapter Eleven

While Jeannie and Noah got ready for school, Katheryn knocked and pushed the door open. She leaned against the door frame, coffee mug in one hand, and a look on her face that meant she was deciding whether to discuss now or later. "Morning, girls. Noah, are you okay?"

"I don't want to talk about it," Noah mumbled behind the sweatshirt she was pulling over her head.

"Well, we're going to talk about it." Katheryn stepped inside. "It's not like you to let some prank set you off like this."

Noah dropped onto the edge of the bed, fingers straightening the hem of her sleeve. "It's not just some prank, Mom. It's been almost every stinking night. Pumpkins, banging on the window, flashlights... I keep having these creepy nightmares about being attacked by some demon jack-o'-lantern. Then I just lie there waiting for whatever he comes up with next."

Jeannie stopped mid-tug on her hair tie and nodded. "She's right. I've seen it too. There's been something like every other night for the last couple of weeks. Nate swears he only did it once, but if that's true, somebody else is behind it."

Katheryn raised an eyebrow. "Who?"

Jeannie shrugged.

"I don't know." Noah avoided her mother's eyes. "I thought if I ignored it, he'd get tired and stop. But now, I feel like I'm going crazy." She threw a pillow at the window. "I can't take any more of his crap."

Katheryn put her coffee on the dresser and sat next to Noah, resting a hand on her shoulder. "Don't say crap. I'll talk to him, but you can't threaten him with a bat anymore. Okay? Just come to us if he does it again."

Noah nodded, but didn't answer. Her heart thudded in her chest, and hot tears burned in her eyes, threatening to spill over any second. Frustration and helplessness churned in her stomach.

The ride to school was unusually quiet. Nate sat in the front passenger seat, arms folded, staring out the window without saying a word. Either their parents had warned him not to, or he wasn't sure what Noah might have to whack him with.

In the back, Noah and Jeannie stared outside, backpacks between their knees. Morning fog hung low in the hollow. The windshield wipers swept away misty droplets every few seconds. Jeannie glanced over at Noah and offered the faintest half-smile. She mimed bonking Nate with an imaginary Louisville Slugger. Noah smiled, bobbing her head as she mouthed the words, "Yes, please."

When they pulled into the drop-off lane, Nate climbed out first, letting the door slam shut as he sprinted to meet his friends. The girls followed, their breath rising into the cold air as they made their way toward the entrance.

The morning dragged on. Math blurred into history. History blurred into science. Noah copied notes from the board without really reading them. Her mind wandered back to the pumpkin and chasing Nate through the yard.

In her mind, she replayed the moment he dropped the jack-o'-lantern. Over and over, she imagined catching him before he could run: the startled look on his face, the satisfying womp of the foam bat connecting with his backside. At most, it would have hurt his pride, but still.

At lunchtime, she repeatedly stabbed her fork into her mashed potatoes. As the only garden-grown food on her plate, they got the blame for the pumpkin shenanigans. Jeannie sat across the table, opening her milk and watching Noah's spud attack. "You okay? I know you're still ticked off," she said.

"Yep," Noah muttered. She wasn't sure if she was okay or not, but she was definitely still ticked off.

Jeannie grinned. "Good. Stay that way. He deserves it."

After lunch, Noah's pulse was back to normal. She no longer fantasized about swinging her bat at Nate's rear end. Not that she'd forgiven him. Far from it. But time and chocolate milk have a way of dulling the edge. By the time art class began, the day felt like just another Monday.

Today's class project was papier-mâché pumpkins. The smell of glue and wet newspaper filled the room. Keeping her hands busy helped Noah forget the morning. Jeannie sat beside her, slapping soggy strips onto a balloon and humming a song Noah didn't recognize.

Jeannie leaned close and grinned. "You should make yours look like Nate's jack-o'-lantern and leave it on his bed."

Noah shot her a look, then snorted. "Yeah, with demon eyes and a tiny baseball bat in its little pumpkin hands."

That made Jeannie laugh so hard her balloon rolled across the table, smearing glue everywhere. The teacher gave them both the keep it down look, but said nothing.

By the time the last bell echoed in the hallway, Noah had mostly cooled off. Walking to the pickup line, her steps were bouncier than they had been that morning, even under the same gloomy gray sky. The next time she saw a jack-o'-lantern in her window, she'd be ready.

Noah spotted Katheryn's SUV in the pickup lane. She jogged toward it with Jeannie beside her. She tossed her backpack into the back seat and slid in after it.

"Where's Nate?" she asked, as her mother pulled the car into drive.

"Dad's picking him up," Katheryn said, easing out of the lane. "I thought we could use a little girl time."

Jeannie's eyebrows lifted. "Where are we going?"

Katheryn smiled at the road ahead. "I thought we'd run to Darla's Diner. You two have had a rough few days, so we're having comfort food for dinner."

Jeannie's eyes lit up. "Even dessert?"

Katheryn laughed. "Oh yeah. Especially dessert."

The smell of diner coffee hit them as soon as they walked in the door. The red vinyl seat squeaked under their jeans as the slid into a booth by the windows. Katheryn ordered coffee and apple strudel, and the girls picked hot chocolate and warm cherry cobbler with double dollops of French vanilla ice cream.

"Excellent choice," Katheryn said. "How did I know that was exactly what you'd order?"

The girls laughed. Noah was happy to hear that sound coming from her mouth. Mom really does know best.

For a while, they ate in silence. The only sounds were the clink of forks and the low hum of the jukebox in the corner. Eventually, Katheryn looked at Noah. "You holding up okay?"

Noah nodded her head. "Better than this morning."

Jeannie nudged her with an elbow. "She didn't threaten Nate all afternoon."

Katheryn's mouth twitched. "That's progress."

Noah shrugged and took another bite of pie. "I'm still not forgiving him."

"Fair enough." Katheryn reached for her coffee. "But I'm proud of you for cooling off. It shows that you have more self-control than he does. But he is your brother, so eventually, you're gonna have to forgive him. Just promise me you'll try to have a normal day tomorrow."

Noah nodded. "I promise."

Walking back to the car, Noah noticed the gray sky, like her mood, had finally lightened. The air itself even smelled fresher, and for the first time all day, Noah wasn't plotting her revenge.

Chapter Twelve

Tuesday morning blew in pale and cold. Fog rimmed the edges of the kitchen windows, and the toaster clicked, as if trying to keep the peace. Noah walked in behind Jeannie and stopped short. Nate sat at the table, hands in his lap like he was in the principal's office.

Katheryn stood by the stove, holding the spatula like a paddle. Will leaned against the counter with his coffee. Nobody was smiling.

Will sipped his coffee. "Good mornin', ladies."

"Morning." Noah slid behind the kitchen table. Jeannie took a seat beside her. The chair legs squeaked on the hardwood, way too loud for how quiet everyone was.

Katheryn set a plate of scrambled eggs in the middle of the table. "Talk," she said, glaring at Nate.

Nate cleared his throat. Eyes down. "So, um … about the jack-o'-lanterns. I'm sorry you got mad."

Noah rolled her eyes and reached for the toast. Her heart was pounding again, despite last night's promise to have a normal day.

Will looked at Nate over the rim of his coffee cup. "How about we try that one more time?"

Nate nodded. "I really am sorry." He blew out a breath. "For the pumpkins, for scaring you, for everything except running from you. You were scary." He stared at his plate. "But I only did it Saturday night and yesterday morning. Cross my heart."

The fork in Noah's hand paused halfway to her plate. "Oh? Yesterday you said you only did it once."

Jeannie tapped Noah's foot under the table, a quiet reminder to breathe.

Noah looked at her father. "It's been way more than twice."

Will nodded. He had expected that part. "Nate has admitted to Saturday night and yesterday morning when you caught him red-handed, but insists the other incidents were not him."

Noah dropped her fork on her plate and crossed her arms. The clatter drew a stern look from her father.

Will held out his palms. "Whether or not that's true, there will be no more pumpkins." Turning back to Nate, he said, "And no more late-night creeping. No more anything that involves windows, jack-o'-lanterns, ghosts, spooky sounds ... none of it. Right?"

"Yes, sir." Nate nodded his head. He sounded small. For a second, Noah almost felt sorry for him.

Katheryn set a glass of orange juice in front of Noah. "And you," she said gently, "do not get to chase anyone with a bat, even a foam one, no matter how wronged you might feel." She held Noah's gaze until Noah nodded. "Good. Now eat before it gets cold."

The tension didn't disappear exactly. It just sat in the corners and cupboards, watching them. Noah took two bites of her eggs and realized she was starving. When she reached for the jelly, she knocked the lid off. It clanked onto the table, wobbling and then flattening like a dropped coin.

"I said I'm sorry," Nate tried again, quieter. "I really mean it."

"Okay," Noah said. It was the best she could do at seven in the morning.

The ride to school was much the same as it had been on Monday. Nate sat in the passenger seat staring out at the gloomy mountain sky. Noah and Jeannie sat in the backseat with their backpacks braced against their knees. Katheryn sang along to Little Buddy Radio but kept a close watch on the twins.

In the drop-off lane, Nate slid out first. He didn't slam the door this time, but he didn't look back either. Noah watched him jog toward the entrance, head down, shoulders hunched against the cold. Jeannie blew a little fog onto the window and drew a smiley face in it with her finger.

"Have a good day, girls," Katheryn said. "I love you both."

"Love you," the girls said, almost in unison as they climbed from the vehicle.

After morning came and went, and lunchtime rolled around, Jeannie traded her cookie for Noah's applesauce. Noah took a bite of the cookie and admitted to herself that her mood was better than yesterday. She wasn't as ticked off, at least. That had to count for something.

"Ready for PE?" Noah asked.

Jeannie made a face. "Ugh. We run the mile today."

"I love to run. I wish we had a track team."

Jeannie gave Noah a look that said, "Have you lost your blasted mind?" Then, cocking her head, she said, "You know what? I kinda do too."

Montcalm Elementary didn't have an actual track. Instead, they ran around the building itself. The crisp autumn air in Noah's lungs refreshed her. She ran a steady four laps, not slow, not fast. When their PE coach yelled their times, she didn't care that hers were in the middle. When Jeannie finished, she flopped onto the grass and announced that she had conquered physical education and was ready for a nap.

By the last bell, the girls were laughing and joking as if nothing had ever happened. The coach was right; this exercise stuff really was good for stress.

In the pickup line, Noah walked up to Nate and hugged him. "You're forgiven."

He eyed her suspiciously. He even seemed to check for a bat.

Katheryn picked them up with the heater going and grocery bags full of what was clearly going to become dinner. "Taco night," she said, but her eyes were a touch misty. She must have seen the hug.

After carrying in the groceries, Noah and Jeannie went straight to the kitchen. Without being asked, they emptied the bags and set the kitchen table.

Will came in a few minutes later and kissed Katheryn on the cheek. Nate hovered by the doorway, then finally edged closer.

"Can I help?" he asked.

"You can grate the cheese," Katheryn said, sliding the block and the grater across the counter. "But try not to grate your knuckles."

Nate made a face. "That's gross, Mom."

She nodded. "Big facts, little dude."

All the kids gave her a look that said, "Ew, she's trying to sound cool again."

Halfway through dinner, Will cleared his throat. "So. Just to revisit the new house rules." He wagged a finger as if he were delivering a sermon. "No pumpkins in the windows. Or sticks near windows. No flashlights pointed at windows. And no creative loopholes. I don't care if it's Halloween, April Fool's Day, or Talk Like a Pirate Day. Clear?"

"Clear," Nate said. He seemed to mean it.

"Clear," Noah echoed. She was pretty tired of arguing and didn't want to be the one who kept it going.

Jeannie lifted her hand. "Do papier-mâché pumpkins count?"

"Only if they're handmade and stay indoors," Will said with a smile.

"Your terms are acceptable," Jeannie said, holding out her hand and shaking Will's.

Nate pushed a piece of cheese around with his fork. "I really am sorry," he said, not looking at anyone. "I know I can be a jerk sometimes, but I really was just trying to be funny."

"I'm sorry too," Noah said, holding out her fist. "Truce?"

"Truce," Nate said, giving it a bump.

Will and Katheryn both watched the exchange, surprise flickering in their faces as the kids made peace. The earlier tension was mostly gone; now everyone could finally breathe again.

After dinner, they did the dishes in a slow, assembly-line fashion. Nate washed, Noah rinsed, Jeannie dried, and Katheryn put away. Will tried to help but got kicked out for using too much water. It was just a normal family evening. Like the kind they had before the Halloween pranks started.

At bedtime, Noah paused at her window. Habit, she guessed. The glass reflected the room like a mirror. Her lamp. Her books on the nightstand. Jeannie pulling her hair into a loose braid. Beyond the reflection, the yard was just a dark slab of withered grass. No glowing eyes—hers, or a pumpkin's.

"Do you think he meant it?" Jeannie asked, climbing into bed. "About being sorry."

"Pretty sure he's sorry he got caught," Noah said. "And sorry I got so mad."

Jeannie laughed. "That's because you get scary."

"Shhh," Noah said, bringing a finger to her lips and winking.

She awoke a few hours later, with that falling sensation you get when a dream tips you back into your body. Still no pumpkin. Still no light. A thin trail of cold air whispered through the tiniest gap at the bottom of the window. When she locked the window, she searched the yard for flashlights, glowing pumpkins, and annoying twin brothers before pulling the curtains shut.

"Go back to sleep," Jeannie mumbled half awake.

"I am," Noah whispered, and she did.

In the morning, She opened the curtains and repeated her scan of the yard—still all clear.

She bowed her head and pressed her hands together. "Just a normal day," she said. "Please?"

Chapter Thirteen

Before getting dressed for school, Noah decided Wednesday was going to be a wonderfully boring kind of day.

At breakfast, Nate wasn't poking at her or making creepy faces over his cereal. He even slid the butter closer when she reached for it.

"Peace offering?"

"Don't push it." The faintest twitch curled the corner of his mouth.

By the time Katheryn pulled into the drop-off line, Noah was in the best mood she'd been in for days.

Hilary was at her locker, leaning in close to Tommy Holloway as he said something that made her laugh. Her hair swung in shiny waves, catching the light like a shampoo commercial. Tommy glanced up when Noah passed, gave her a quick nod, then went right back to whatever joke he was telling. She might kind of like him, off and on, but even Hilary wasn't going to ruin her day.

In art class, the tables were pushed together in clusters, each topped with half-finished papier-mâché pumpkins from the day before. The smell of tempera paint hit them the moment they walked in. Balloons, now hardened under layers of newspaper and glue, sat waiting for their first coats of orange, green, or whatever wild color people had decided on.

Noah dropped into her seat, spinning her pumpkin so the smoothest side faced her. She dipped a wide brush into orange paint and pulled the first stroke across the lumpy surface.

"Looks like a basketball." Jeannie dabbed green streaks onto her pumpkin's stem.

"That's because yours is neon green."

"Artistic vision," Jeannie replied. "You wouldn't understand."

Across the room, Hilary's pumpkin was already half covered in a perfect, even layer of gold paint. Tommy was helping her. A smear of gold paint ran down her sleeve. Jeannie caught Noah glancing at them and huffing.

"I thought you said you didn't like him."

"I don't." Noah slapped on another stripe of orange paint. "That gold makes her pumpkin look like a Christmas ornament."

Jeannie grinned. "You should tell her that."

"Hard pass."

By the time class was over, Noah's pumpkin looked more pumpkin-y than basketball-y. She and Jeannie carried them to the drying rack and headed back to class.

The rest of the day was a blur of assignments and quizzes. The bell rang, and students spilled into the hall. As Noah slung her backpack over one shoulder, she stood waiting for Jeannie, but ahead, a scene was unfolding near the exit door.

As Hilary was zipping her backpack, Brooke Sutter from the other sixth-grade class closed in with two of her friends in tow.

Brooke was like the typical mean girl you see in all the teen movies. Her friends were more like minions.

"Well, if it isn't Princess Glitter," Brooke said, eyeing Hilary's gold-streaked sleeve. "Want me to paint your face to match your pumpkin?"

Hilary stiffened. "Go away, Brooke."

Brooke shoved her against the wall. "Why? I'm just curious if your tiara's in your backpack or if you left it at home." Her friends giggled as if on cue.

Noah saw Hilary's shoulders slump and her eyes grow misty. She might not have been a big Hilary fan, but there was no way she was going to stand by and watch her get bullied. In three fast strides, she was standing between them.

"You're being a bully, Brooke. Knock it off."

Brooke put her hands on her hips. "Or what?"

"Or you and I are going to have a big problem."

Brooke's minions flanked her. "One of you and three of us. I guess I'm not seeing the problem."

Jeannie rushed over, dropping her backpack with a thud and planting herself shoulder-to-shoulder with Noah. "Your problems just doubled."

Brooke tilted her head. "What, are you Noah's body-guard now?"

"She doesn't need a bodyguard. I'm just trying to keep her from getting detention for kicking your butt."

Brooke and her friends moved toward Noah and Jean-nie.

Noah stepped forward, placing her left foot a double shoulder's width ahead of her right in a defensive stance her dad had taught her. She brought her fists up to chest level. Her eyes narrowed in determination.

Brooke looked surprised that someone, anyone, had the gall to confront her. Her smirk faltered. "Whatever. Go build an ark." She flicked her hair back and led her friends toward the buses.

Hilary let out a breath. "Thanks, Noah. You didn't have to do that."

"I know," Noah said as she and Jeannie walked her to the pickup line. "But my dad always says you can't go around a bully. You have to meet them head-on. That takes away their power."

Hilary nodded. "But they'll just come back when you're not around."

"Maybe," Noah said. "But if they do, you're strong enough to stand up to them."

For a second, Hilary looked like she might smile, but then her eyes darted, as if looking for Brooke. "I guess."

When they got in the car, Jeannie was laughing hysterically. "Did you see the look on Brooke's face when you stepped toward her instead of backing up?"

"Noah?" Katheryn turned, shaking her head. "What did you do?"

"Nothing, Mom," Noah said, shushing Jeannie.

Getting in the car, Nate's expression was one of sheer delight. "Did you really beat up Brooke and her little playmates?"

"NOAH!" Katheryn shouted from the driver's seat.

"Mom, I swear I didn't touch them. I just stood up to them for trying to bully Hilary, and they backed down. Dad always says, never let anyone get bullied."

"You would have been proud, Mrs. James. Noah went all bad booty on them."

"Uh, I had help," Noah said, raising Jeannie's hand like she'd won a wrestling match.

"Girls. What am I going to do with you?" Katheryn looked mortified.

On the drive home, Noah and Jeannie giggled every time they looked at one another.

Noah's stomach rumbled as she walked into the kitchen. Katheryn was pulling a tray of garlic bread from the oven, and Mattey Marshall was helping Nate set the table. The James house was sort of the unofficial Spook Hollow hangout.

"Hey, Doc," he said when Noah walked in. "Survived another day?"

"Why?" Jeannie asked, wrinkling her eyebrows. "What did you hear?"

"Huh?"

"Never mind," Noah said, swatting at Jeannie.

Dinner was comfortably loud and fun. Nate told a story he had heard on the Synaptic Misfires YouTube channel about a camp counselor who got lost in a haunted cave. Mattey matched it with one about a psychic detective who ran screaming from a mummy at a crime scene. By dessert—apple turnover with vanilla ice cream—Noah was leaning back in her chair, full and warm and not thinking about pumpkins or bullies.

That night, she fell asleep quickly. A heavy, dreamless kind of sleep that came after a good day. After midnight, a soft thump woke her. She lay still, eyes open in the dark. A second thump followed, closer this time, like something shifting against the side of the house.

She listened, waiting for Lord knows what to happen, but nothing else did. The only sounds were the hum of the refrigerator downstairs and the faint tick of the clock in the hall. She pulled the blanket tighter and told herself it was the wind, or maybe a trash can had blown over.

She didn't look out the window, but the uneasy prickle running down her spine kept her eyes open longer than usual.

Chapter Fourteen

Sunlight streamed through the kitchen windows, casting warm golden rectangles across the breakfast table. Noah sat buttering her toast, enjoying a peaceful morning. Last night brought no mysterious pumpkins, no glowing eyes, no creepy nightmares, and no wanting to wring Nate's neck. But as they say, the day was young.

"Pass the syrup, Nozie," Nate said, already halfway through his second stack of pancakes.

"Get it yourself, Natezie," she barked, but with no real bite. She was in too good a mood to pick a fight.

"My hands are full." He held up his fork and knife like evidence.

Jeannie shook her head and slid the syrup bottle across the table. "There. Crisis averted."

"Thanks, Jeannie. See, Noah? God wants us to help each other." Nate grinned and drowned his pancakes in maple syrup.

"Yes, but God doesn't want us to enable each other." Noah took a bite of her toast. "You've got perfectly good arms."

"Speaking of good arms." Nate rolled up the sleeve of his T-shirt and flexed a skinny bicep. "Wait until you see how buff I get from all the hiking and stuff at camp. I'll probably come back looking like The Rock."

Noah chuckled. "More like The Pebble."

"Ha ha. You're hilarious. But seriously, we're going to do archery and canoeing on the lake, and they have this rope course that's like thirty feet high..."

"Eat your breakfast, Nowayne Johnson," Will interrupted from behind his coffee mug. "You've got about five hours before I pick you up at school."

"Four hours and forty-eight minutes," Nate corrected, checking the countdown timer on his 'survival' watch. "Not that I'm counting or anything."

Katheryn laughed as she flipped another batch of pancakes. "Oh, no. I can tell you're not excited at all."

"I packed and repacked my bag like four times yesterday," Nate admitted. "I keep thinking I'm forgetting something important."

"Like what?" Jeannie asked.

Nate shrugged. "I don't know. That's the problem. What if it's something I don't realize I need until I need it and don't have it?"

"Isn't that the whole point of being a scout? Learning to live off nature's land and all that?" Noah teased, saluting him. It was the sisterly thing to do. But if she was being honest, she had to admit, it was nice seeing Nate this happy about something that didn't involve jumping out of her closet or pulling pranks. He'd been talking about scout camp for weeks.

"You've got everything on the packing list," Will assured him. "Plus about ten things that aren't."

"Hey, you never know when you might need an extra compass, whistle, or paracord," Nate said defensively.

Noah rolled her eyes playfully. "Paracord? Dad!"

Will laughed. "We paratroopers call it suspension line, son. Get it right or you're not going," he said with mock sternness.

"He's joking," Katheryn said quickly. "Nate, honey, you have everything you'll need. Trust me."

After breakfast, Nate disappeared upstairs to check his bag one last time while the girls gathered their backpacks and homework folders.

"Come on, gang!" Katheryn called from the kitchen. "Time to go!"

On the ride to school, Nate rambled non-stop about scout camp. He'd already told them about the rope course and the lake twice, but apparently, had more details to share.

Noah stared out the window at the Bluestone River and the familiar trees and houses that drifted past the car. Everything looked so normal this morning. Even the jack-o'-lanterns on people's porches looked friendly and festive. Maybe she really had just let her imagination run wild.

As the blue Montcalm Generals sign came into view, Nate was still talking. "...and they have this zipline that goes out over the trees. He bounced in his seat. "You wear a harness and everything. It's totally safe, but it looks super dangerous."

"Sounds terrifying," Jeannie said.

"Sounds awesome," Nate corrected. "I can't wait."

At school, Nate immediately started telling anyone who would listen about his upcoming adventure. During the morning announcements, the teacher called him out for talking to his seatmate.

"If your dad doesn't get Nate to Pipestem soon, his head is going to explode," Jeannie whispered during math class.

"I know. He's like a squirrel on a sugar rush. I've never seen him this wound up about anything." Noah erased a wrong answer and tried to focus on long division. "It's kind of nice, though. At least he's too distracted to be a pain."

The morning passed quickly. Noah actually enjoyed her classes without constantly worrying about the pranks Nate might have planned for her. During recess, she and Jeannie sat on the swings and talked about their plans for Halloween night.

"Mom texted; I can definitely stay the whole weekend," Jeannie said, pumping her legs to swing higher. "She and Dad are picking me up long enough for campaign pictures at the pumpkin patch." She stuck a finger in her mouth, mock gagging herself.

Noah laughed. "Perfect. We can watch movies and eat all the candy we want. Without Nate trying to scare us."

Jeannie gave Noah a single exaggerated head nod. "Exactly."

Just before lunch, the school secretary's voice came over the intercom. "Nathaniel James, and Matthew Marshall, please come to the office. You have an early dismissal."

Excitement fluttered through Noah. Nate was really leaving and wouldn't be back until after Halloween. The pumpkin pranks were definitely over.

A few minutes later, she saw Nate and Mattey walking past her classroom window with Will. Nate caught sight of her through the glass and gave her a huge grin and a thumbs-up.

Noah waved and smiled. She was genuinely happy for him.

The rest of the school day flew by. During art class, they put the finishing touches on their paper-mâché pumpkins. Noah painted a friendly jack-o'-lantern with a big, toothless smile and yellow triangle eyes. It looked nothing like the creepy one Nate carved to mess with her.

"That's really cute," Jeannie said, adding orange paint to her own pumpkin. "Very non-terrifying."

"That's the idea."

After school, Noah and Jeannie carried their pumpkins to the pickup line. The late October air was cool, crisp, and perfect for Halloween. Orange and red leaves drifted in the breeze. The mountains around Spook Hollow blazed with autumn colors.

Katheryn was waiting, just like always.

"Hi, girls. How was school?"

"Good," Noah said, climbing into the back seat. "Are Dad and Nate already at camp?"

"Yep. They should be setting up their tents right about now. Your father texted me about thirty minutes ago."

Noah smiled. Nate, and his pranks, were gone. The weekend was going to be perfect.

At home, she and Jeannie spread out on the living room carpet with a deck of cards. Noah's parents had a firm rule: for every hour of screen time, there had to be two hours of no screens. The house was wonderfully quiet without Nate's constant noise and energy.

"Crazy Eights or Uno?" Jeannie asked, holding a deck of cards in each hand.

"Crazy Eights. After I win, I pick the PlayStation game."

"Mmm hmm." Jeannie passed out the cards like a Las Vegas poker dealer.

They played cards and talked about school, Halloween plans, and which flavor of popcorn salt they should use for their Halloween movie night.

"Who said we can only use one?"

Noah had missed this kind of conversation while she'd been watching windows and jumping at shadows.

"I can't believe how quiet it's been since Nate stopped all his pranks," she said, arranging her cards. "But I'm not complaining."

"Maybe your parents really did scare him straight," Jeannie suggested.

"Maybe." Noah played the eight of hearts, changing the suit. "It's just nice not having to worry about what he's going to do next, you know? I've been sleeping so much better."

"I noticed. You haven't woken me up screaming about killer pumpkins in a couple of days."

Noah's cheeks warmed. "Yeah, sorry about that. I guess between Nate and my imagination, I let things get out of hand."

"It happens. Remember when I was convinced my neighbor's cat was actually a demon in disguise?"

Noah nodded. "Well, that cat is pretty creepy."

"Right? Those eyes are way too spooky for a regular cat."

Around five o'clock, Will called.

"How's camp going?" Katheryn asked, putting her phone on speaker.

"Good. Nate is so excited I practically had to tie him to a tree." Will laughed. "He's having a great time."

"And we're going to have a quiet weekend," Noah shouted from the living room.

"That you are," Will agreed.

After Noah, Jeannie, and Katheryn shared the details of their day, he said, "Well, duty calls. Time to teach Campfire 101. I love you guys."

"Love you," Noah and Katheryn said in unison.

Jeannie looked down at her hands. "That's really nice. The way you guys always tell each other that. Even on the phone."

Noah nodded, understanding her meaning. Jeannie's family wasn't big on affection. "Yeah, it is. But, you know we love you just like family."

Jeannie smiled and squeezed Noah's hand in return. "Backatcha."

From the kitchen, Katheryn's voice rang out. "What do you girls want for dinner? Since it's just us, want to DoorDash a pizza?"

"Yes, please!" Both girls shouted at the same time.

As evening settled over Spook Hollow, they ate pizza and, instead of PlayStation, watched a teen comedy on TV. Something that had nothing to do with pumpkins or scares.

Later, as she got ready for bed, Noah looked out her window at the quiet yard below. No glowing eyes. No creepy grins, just a normal October night.

Tomorrow was Friday the 31st, kind of the opposite of Friday the 13th. But it was Halloween, and speaking of opposites, for the first time, Nate wouldn't be there to spook her. She was a little sad they wouldn't be together on his favorite holiday, but maybe this Halloween would be all about tricks and treats instead of torment and terror. So, what could go wrong?

Chapter Fifteen

F RIDAY AT 3:10 PM, the school bell rang. Halloween had officially begun. Noah and Jeannie dropped off their books and hurried outside to meet Katheryn in the pickup line.

The crisp October air was cool enough for light jackets, but the afternoon sun felt warm. Leaves crunched under their sneakers as they joined the crowd of kids heading home for the weekend.

"Hi, ladies. How was school?" Katheryn asked with a smile.

As usual, her SUV was loaded with supplies she'd picked up for the homeless shelter. Boxes of canned goods and warm blankets filled the back—another afternoon spent serving others.

"Hi, Mrs. James," Jeannie said with a smile.

Noah reached through the open window and hugged her mother. "It was good. How was your day?"

"It's been good. Busy, but good," she said, smiling from ear to ear.

"Come here, Jeannie." Katheryn held out her arms, and Jeannie reached through the window for a hug.

On the ride home, Noah watched leaves swirl across the road in colorful spirals. She loved this time of year, but other than tubing at Winterplace, she wasn't the least bit excited about the cold winter peeking around the corner. She wished the mountains around Spook Hollow would keep their color until spring.

Katheryn glanced in the rear-view mirror. "Are you sure you girls don't want to trick-or-treat?"

"Mom! We're too old for that," Noah groaned from the back seat.

"No, you're not, but okay," Katheryn said, raising a hand in surrender.

"We're dressing up to give out candy, though," Jeannie chimed in, excited.

When they arrived at home, Noah and Jeannie decorated the front porch with black lights, straw bales, and a speaker playing spooky sounds to attract ghouls, ghosts, goblins, and all manner of trick-or-treaters.

Before the dew fell and twilight painted the sky purple and orange, they headed into the warm house. The living room smelled faintly of cinnamon candle.

"What movie did you girls pick?" Katheryn called from the kitchen as she finished loading the dishwasher.

"Hocus Pocus," Noah called back, already settling onto the couch. "Jeannie's never seen it."

"Really?" Katheryn poked her head around the corner. "Oh, you're in for a treat, Jeannie. Just don't blame me if you have nightmares about witches on flying vacuum cleaners."

"Mom!" Noah threw up her hands, while Jeannie's eyes widened slightly.

"It's not that scary," Noah assured her. "It's more funny than scary."

Jeannie adjusted the wizard hat on her head as she flopped onto the floor.

"Easy there, Hermione Stranger. You'll bruise your wand," Noah teased.

"Says the girl whose costume is a doctor coat and stethoscope." Jeannie shot back with a wave of her wand and something that sounded remotely spell-like.

Noah pulled a syringe from her white-coat pocket. "Hush, or you're getting a shot."

They nestled on the floor against the couch with a bowl of popcorn between them and a pile of pillows and blankets. Outside, darkness had settled over Spook Hollow, making the glow of the TV and the low-burning fireplace the only sources of light in the cozy living room.

As the opening credits rolled and the spooky singing began, Noah settled back, ready for a perfect night with her best friend.

Every so often, the doorbell rang, and the girls jumped up to hand out candy and talk to kids before racing back to the movie.

During a particularly spooky scene where a zombie chased the kids and cat through Salem's sewers, Jeannie grabbed Noah's arm. "This is scarier than you said!"

"It gets less scary," Noah whispered back, though she found herself glancing toward the dark window behind them. The flickering light from the TV made strange shadows dance across the glass.

When the Sanderson sisters went up in eerie green smoke at the high school, Jeannie buried her face in a pillow. "Tell me when this part's over."

"You're gonna miss the part where they turn back into witches." Noah laughed, pulling the blanket higher around both of them.

Jeannie turned to her with a confused expression. "Wait. How did they turn back into witches after they got kilned?"

Noah laughed. "Kilned? What does that even mean?"

"You know," Jeannie said. "Killed in the pottery kiln."

Noah shrugged. "Magic?"

"Yes! Hollywood magic," Katheryn chimed in with a wink.

Jeannie nodded, engrossed in the film. Her parents rarely did family things like just sitting with her and watching movies, so when Jeannie stayed over, the James family tried to make up for the things she missed out on.

"Look at that one," Jeannie pointed at the screen, where a particularly menacing jack-o'-lantern sat on a porch step. "His smile is all messed up."

"Like it's missing a tooth," Noah observed, though something about the image twisted her stomach in knots.

As the movie continued, Noah found herself thinking about the pumpkin. THE pumpkin...

By the time the closing credits rolled, both girls were fast asleep. They missed the last part of the movie.

"Sistas," Katheryn said, waking them in her witchiest voice. "It's bedtime."

The girls stumbled upstairs, changed into pajamas, and brushed their teeth. Katheryn poked her head in to say goodnight, reminding them to keep the noise down since it was getting late.

"Sweet dreams, you two," she said, clicking off the overhead light. "Don't let the bedbugs bite."

"Or the witches," Jeannie added sleepily, making Noah giggle.

Before long, they were fast asleep.

Just before midnight, Noah's eyes snapped open. Something was off. The house was completely silent. No creaking floorboards, no distant sounds, no familiar nighttime noises. Even the furnace seemed to be holding its breath.

Her finger throbbed with the same sharp, rhythmic pulse that had been coming and going for days, and a soft orange light filled the room. An unsteady, unnatural flickering that caused shadows to writhe and twist across her ceiling like gnarled witch fingers.

Her chest tightened.

Slowly, she turned her head toward the window.

It was there.

Eyes glowing brighter than ever, like tiny forest fires. That jagged, crooked, sneering grin.

The jack-o'-lantern sat perfectly still outside her window, pressing against the glass and staring straight at her. But now she could see it more clearly, the way its carved features seemed deeper, darker. Fire shot through the missing tooth gap.

Noah's breath caught in her throat. She shut her eyes and counted to three.

One... throb

Two... throb

Three... throb

She opened her eyes. It was still there. She pinched herself. Ouch.

The pumpkin was still watching, still smiling that terrible, broken smile.

The worst part? She could swear the pumpkin's grin had gotten wider since she'd last looked. And that awful flickering behind those hollow eye sockets... The orange glow pulsed like a beating heart made entirely of fire.

Throb-throb. Her finger pulsed in perfect rhythm with the pumpkin's glow. Throb-throb. The orange streak on her finger flared too—brighter with each pulse. Throb-throb. The harder her heart pounded, the brighter the fire behind those sinister eyes grew. As if some invisible force connected them.

In the glowing light, dark lines spread across the pumpkin's face, swelling into veins and throbbing in perfect time with the beating flame inside. Each beat made the carved face seem more alive, more aware, more impossibly wrong.

The pumpkin face pushed harder against the window with every fiery beat. The glass bulged inward like a pumpkin-shaped bubble ready to burst. The window frame creaked under the pressure, but the glass held, warping and stretching but refusing to break. With each throb, the pumpkin's face seemed to push closer. The orange glow grew brighter, more intense.

Gooey, black liquid oozed from the pumpkin's jagged mouth. It slid down the glass in thick, sticky ribbons. The shadowy goo didn't behave like a normal liquid. It moved with purpose, creeping in perfectly straight lines toward the bottom of the window frame. It seeped under the closed window like smoke, defying physics as it poured through the impossibly thin gap between the sash and sill.

The dark ooze hit the floor and spread out in tendrils. Pooling, no, crawling across her bedroom in a deliberate search. It left an oily stain on everything it touched. A sick-sweet stench hit her nose, the smell of warm, rotting pumpkin guts.

Noah watched in helpless horror as the creeping, crawling shadow goo reached the foot of her bed. In the wall mirror, she watched it slither up the footboard, defying gravity. Inch by inch, it crept higher, closer. Noah tried to wake Jeannie, but she was too terrified to move. Too terrified to scream.

With each throb of her finger, with each pulse of that nightmarish light, she sunk deeper into paralysis. The ooze kept coming, surrounding her.

The fire inside the pumpkin was blazing now, threatening to melt the glass. A hairline fracture appeared in the center of the bulging window. And it was spreading.

The ooze wrapped around her body, cocooning her. One tendril moved over her cross necklace, pushing it into her skin. It reminded Noah of her father's sermon, and of standing up to Brooke just days before: *Bullies just want to scare you.*

The warmth of the cross broke her paralysis. She could move. She could speak. The tendrils binding her loosened. She could fight back.

She turned her head to stare directly into the fiery eyes at the window. Her voice was steady and calm. She shook her head. "And I'm not afraid of you anymore."

The glowing grin faltered. The orange glow weakened as her pulse slowed.

You can't go around bullies. You have to meet them head on.

"You don't have the power to hurt me. And you can't scare me, either." Noah's voice grew stronger and more confident. "So get out."

The jack-o'-lantern's glow darkened. Its carved features deflated like a popped balloon, but it didn't move.

Noah drew in a deep lungful of air. "I said GET OUT!" she shouted at the top of her lungs.

As the hollow eyes dimmed to pixel points, the dark ooze swirled back under the window sash and into the darkness like a flushing toilet. The bulging window snapped back into shape as the pumpkin flew away, vanishing into the night.

Jeannie leaped from the bed, her expression was one of pure terror as Katheryn rushed through the door shouting their names, "Noah, Jeannie, what's going on?"

After gathering herself, Noah told them about how the pumpkin had attacked her, and how she had defeated it.

"There's nothing out there, sweetie. You woke yourself up screaming. It was all just a bad dream." Her mother hugged her. "Nothing to worry about."

After the last couple of weeks, Noah didn't trust herself to know what was real and what wasn't. Could it have all been a dream?

It sure didn't feel like it, but dream or no dream, she and Jeannie spent the night in Katheryn's room. They didn't wake until late morning.

When the girls came downstairs, Noah noticed the creeping orange scar on her finger was completely gone, as if nothing strange had ever happened.

She convinced herself that the whole thing had been a combination of her overactive imagination, Nate's pumpkin pranks, and all those freaky dreams. Together, they had tricked her into believing in demonic pumpkins.

There couldn't have been a jack-o'-lantern staring in her window, dripping slime that could actually climb onto her bed and wrap her like a mummy. That was way too weird, even for Spook Hollow.

After breakfast, her mother went upstairs to gather laundry. A few minutes later, she returned carrying a clothes hamper. "Noah, I was just in your room. What in the world happened to your window?"

Noah's stomach lurched into her throat. She knew she could never unhear her mother's next words.

"It's cracked."

www.ingramcontent.com/pod-product-compliance
Lightning Source LLC
Chambersburg PA
CBHW050455110726
47899CB00003B/948